Patience and Courage

Patience and Courage

Book Two: The Survival Instinct

Rachel Bramble

JANUS PUBLISHING COMPANY
London, England

First published in Great Britain 2009
by Janus Publishing Company Ltd,
105–107 Gloucester Place,
London W1U 6BY

www.januspublishing.co.uk

British Library Cataloguing-in-Publication Data
A catalogue record for this book is available from the British Library

ISBN 978-1-85756-646-8

Cover Design: Janus Publishing

Printed and bound in Great Britain

Dedication

To Sheila who has worked as
a social worker for 35 years and has
not received any recognition.

Chapter One

"I've lost the baby," Steph screamed down the phone to John. "Now Alan has gone forever and I have nothing."

"Is your mum there?" said John.

"Yes."

"That's good." John wanted to make sure that Steph had support.

He had been in the middle of getting the final list of directions for his latest script and been out with Clare the night before. He felt a bit annoyed by Steph's call. Since Alan and Paul had died Steph had been on the phone to him all of the time. She was going to work but not managing very well. He felt pulled between Steph, his personal life and his work.

"Look Steph, you'll just have to move up here with me, you ring me all the time and I can't do any work."

"I'm sorry it's just …" Steph put down the phone.

John had always said that he would be there for her but now she knew that she would just have to pull herself together. Alan was dead and she couldn't get him back. She had seen too many people who had given up and she wasn't about to be one of them.

John was cross with himself. He had planned to see Clare tonight. He rang her and said that he had to go to Birmingham.

"Oh, its Steph again, is it?" Clare snapped at him.

Clare was a beautiful woman with a good brain but she also had a coldness about her. When he had talked to her about what Steph did as a job she had said that she could never do that and that families should look after their own. She was from a fairly wealthy family and as far as he knew had not had any money worries.

He thought of Steph and how loyal she was to Alan but he hadn't turned out to be as honest as he had made out. He had left Steph with huge debts and she had had to sell both his and her house; to clear the debts.

She didn't have enough money to put down a deposit for a mortgage and so was now back living with her parents.

It hurt so much, she felt so alone. She didn't want to bother John but she just couldn't get by without him. Every night she cried herself to sleep. She had had a month off work after they died but she had just hidden away from the world.

John had come down every weekend to see her. Often she would fall asleep in his arms and wake to find herself alone as he slept on the settee. Her parents knew that he was an honourable man and would not take advantage of her. But now she had gone too far and chased him away forever. It was Friday and she got up after yet another restless night and got ready for work.

She dabbed her eyes with the familiar flannel which she had used for the last four months and then brushed her hair, which had lost its lustre. She looked in the mirror and said to herself, "Steph this is no good, life must go on."

She knew that she had to make a new start and today she was doing that.

John drove down the motorway and was cross with himself. How could he get annoyed with Steph. She had done so much for him when he had been low and was always there for him and now in return he found it so hard seeing her distressed. When he held her in his arms, rocking her to sleep she seemed so vulnerable and yet also she turned him on. He wanted her so much but could just never tell her. It seemed indecent. Alan had only been dead a few weeks when he started to feel this way.

Her parents had told him that he should get on with his life but what was life without Steph. However hard he tried to find new women in his life they just didn't live up to her.

The motorway was very busy and he felt tired. It was 6pm and he still had only reached Stafford; he stopped at Stafford services to ring Stephs parents.

"Hi, look I'll have something to eat here," he said.

"Steph isn't home yet."

"Is she allright?"

2

"She's got some children that she's had to take into care."

John ate his soup and roll. He wasn't sure what it was meant to be but it was warm and filling. He hadn't had much to eat over the last few weeks with concentrating on deadlines and worrying about Steph. Friends had worried that he looked rather thin.

He was making some good friends in Manchester. He had traced some of his old school friends and had joined a local folk group and made some friends through that. Moving back to Manchester had been a good move and he was beginning to become a little more solvent. He had moved out of the rented flat and had bought himself a small semi-detached house that needed doing up. He had never really been a handyman purely because he had enough money to get people to do jobs for him but now he found that he had a talent which he never knew about.

As he drove again he thought of the wiring job that he planned to do over the weekend. The whole house needed rewiring and he was gradually doing each room. He was learning what to do from reading a manual and had an electrician friend who checked it from time to time.

The motorway seemed to be flowing a bit quicker and as seven o'clock approached he headed for the city centre. He would be in Northfield within half an hour.

Chapter Two

"I'm going to do it," said the young woman as she sat with her child on the edge of the block of flats.

"Nobody can persuade me this time. You social lot have done bugger all for me, you with all your airs and graces and so perfect children and lives."

Steph stood next to the policewoman. She couldn't take any more and started to walk away.

"And where are you going?" the young woman said. "Home to your darling husband?"

This was it, Steph had had enough.

"Get off there," she ordered.

"Oh, you can speak then," said the woman.

"You don't know the hell what you are talking about."

"Steph leave it," said the policewoman.

"No, let her speak, here, you can have her," the young woman handed her baby to the policewoman.

"I suppose now you'll let me jump, now you've got my kid. You only want to take her off me anyhow."

"You, you, you," said Steph, "what about her? She deserves a life."

"But I don't, that's what you are saying?"

"I'm not saying that at all, you just drove me mad that's all. I'm tired, hungry and want to go home but I'm not going until I know you are OK."

"So you better ring your fella and tell him you are going to be late."

Steph ignored her. There was just no point.

"Tell me about him," the young woman said. "Someone like you must have one, or are you like those nosy social workers who expects the likes of me to tell you everything and we get nothing in exchange. I've come across some real bitches in my time."

"I'm sorry if you have," Steph said, softening her tone. "I'm sorry but I can't tell you my life."

"Why?" said the woman.

"Because it hurts too much."

"If I come down from here will you tell me?"

"I'm not sure if I can."

The young woman climbed down and came towards Steph.

"What is so awful that you can't tell ... look I'll make us a coffee, do you want a fag?"

The policewoman had returned.

"I don't want her around, only you."

"OK," said Steph.

"Ring me," said Shirley, the policewoman.

"Yes," said Steph.

Steph and the young woman climbed down the fire escape, entered the main entrance to the block of flats and then took the lift to the sixth floor.

The young woman unlocked the door as if nothing had happened, went into the kitchen and put on the kettle. "Tea or coffee?" she said as she lit her cigarette.

"Only water for me," said Steph.

"So tell me then," said the young woman and so Steph did.

She told this stranger about her love for Alan and the years until they got together and how wonderful those few months had been with Alan and Paul. She told her how she had become pregnant and had found out just a few days before it had happened. She had everything that she ever wanted and then suddenly it was all gone.

"Oh, that's awful," the young woman said, "and I was worrying about my life."

"And now I am living back at home."

"And when is the baby due?"

"I lost it," Steph said and she suddenly realised that she could talk about it all without crying.

She found it soothing talking to this complete stranger and they began to talk woman to woman about all sorts of things.

"Have you done that before?" Steph said.

"Yes," said Nicky.

Steph had found out her name and Nicky had told Steph things that she said that she had never told anyone else.

"So did you really want to die or were you just avoiding things?"

"I don't know."

"You have helped me a lot tonight," said Steph. "I know that Alan and Paul would want me to be happy, but it's so hard. I have to survive."

"You are so open, Steph, I wish you were my social worker, she is a bitch."

"Perhaps if you talked to her differently she wouldn't be; try it when you see her again."

"I'll try."

Steph's mobile rang. It was the policewoman.

"She's checking you are OK?" said Nicky.

"Yes," said Steph.

"I would never hurt anyone," said Nicky.

"Well, prove it then," said Steph. "It's late, I need to go home, the police have put Sarah with foster parents tonight under a Police Protection Order. Your social worker will be in touch with you tomorrow."

"Will they let me have her back, Steph?"

"Nicky, you need to get your act together. If you really want Sarah you have to prove it, you have to work with people."

"I would if it was you," she said.

"Until there was something I did that you didn't like," said Steph. "I've got to go."

Steph went down in the lift with some young lads who looked like they were going for a night on the town. She suddenly felt very old. She had been advised to rest for a few days after losing the baby but she had had so much time off work since Alan had died that her cases were getting in a mess. "It's you that matters," Martin had said, "we'll manage." But moping at home had done her no good.

She suddenly remembered that John was coming. She shouldn't have panicked. She shouldn't have rung him. He had a new woman in his life who he seemed to be very keen on. She wasn't being fair to him.

Chapter Three

John had always got on well with Steph's parents. On one occasion a few weeks before Steph had married Alan, Steph's dad had taken him aside and asked him whether she was marrying the right man.

"You really love my daughter, don't you?" he had said with a knowing look in his eye.

"She has chosen a good man," he had replied.

"Yes," Steph's dad had said, and never mentioned it again.

But it was true, he had really loved Steph, and now as he sat with Steph's parents he thought how different it would be if it had been him that she had chosen. But then he would probably still be in Birmingham and would not be doing all the interesting work that he was doing in Manchester.

They had started filming the pilot of the TV series, which was going to be called The Team. Steph had thought that it was a bit naff as it could mean any kind of team. She wanted something more powerful, like Pride without Prejudice. But then she was looking from a completely different angle to him. He wanted to let the public know what people like Steph did every day but she thought that it should be more from the angle of the relationship between social work and the media.

"It could be like your life and mine," she had said but that was before Alan died. He hadn't talked to Steph about the programme since Alan's death. If the pilot went well they would go ahead with the series, otherwise it would be shelved, Brian had told him.

It was nearly eleven o'clock when Steph rang home to say that she was just leaving and would be home in about half an hour. She drove home. It was a dreary night and suddenly Steph felt very hungry and tired. She had lost a lot of weight over the last few weeks. She just couldn't be bothered to eat but now she felt ravenous.

She would often cry in the car on her way home from work. She would talk to Alan aloud, asking him why he wasn't still with her and saying that she missed him so much but tonight she smiled and told him that she would be OK. Perhaps she would never be as happy again as she had been for those few weeks that she had had as a family but she would survive.

She had the survival instinct and she would help others to gain it too.

One worker who she didn't know very well had said that she would find someone else and be happy again, but others had frowned as she had said this as if to say that she may never be happy again but tonight seeing a woman so desperate, so lonely, Steph thought, "I have to survive for that woman and her child's sake."

She parked the car in the drive. The lights from the house seemed warm and welcoming.

"Hello you," said John as he hugged Steph.

"We're off," said Steph's dad. "Night love," he said as he kissed Steph on the cheek.

"Night Dad," she said and then gave her mum a big hug.

"Don't stay up too late, you two," said Mum.

"We won't," said John.

"I'm starving," said Steph as she opened a tin of tomato soup and poured some into a bowl. "Do you want some?" she asked John.

"No," he said.

Steph slurped her soup and dipped her buttered toast into it.

"So?" she said.

"So what?" said John.

"How is Clare and how is the filming going?"

"Both fine," he said.

"Is that all?"

John realised that Steph, for the first time for weeks, seemed like her old self.

Steph put her bowl, plate, knife and spoon into the dishwasher. Her parents had done without one for years but when Steph sold her house she brought the dishwasher with her and in just a few weeks everyone had got used to using it.

"So how are you feeling?" John asked.

"You mean after the miscarriage?" she said.

"Yes, and generally."

"I'll survive," she said.

"You'll always survive," he said, "it's part of your nature."

Steph suddenly had this great urge; she leapt towards John and kissed him.

"What are you doing?" he said.

"Make love to me," Steph said. "I just want to feel that warm closeness again."

"I can't," he said.

"Why? Is it Clare, my parents?"

"No, I just can't."

"But I thought you loved me; if it wasn't Alan, it would have been you, you know that."

"Yes, but Steph, you will find someone else and I will be second best, I just can't."

John lay on the settee. He had wanted Steph so much. A couple of years ago he would have jumped eagerly but now he just couldn't, he realised that his life had truly moved on and Steph was no longer a significant part of it. He never wanted to be second best again.

Chapter Four

There were three children involved in the case. It was a new one to the team and it was just bad luck that Steph had got it on a Friday. She had only just started back on the duty rota and the day had been quiet until Grove Park School rang at 2.30pm to say that they were concerned about Jamie and Luke's safety. The assessment team had been involved briefly when the children's father had beaten their mother up and Luke, who was eight, had got caught in the tussle trying to protect his mother. Their father had agreed to live away from the family and a few days later had been arrested for GBH. He was now in prison but the children's mum had found a new chap who seemed to be as equally violent as their father. He had come to school that day and threatened a teacher. The children had spoken of their fear of going home and Luke had been disruptive on and off for most of the week.

Steph checked the computer records to see if the new boyfriend was known at all and found nothing on the local record. According to the headteacher he came from Blackpool and so Steph rang the Blackpool office.

"Oh no, not him," was the response of the duty officer. "He is well known to us and is a schedule one offender." Steph knew that this meant that he had been convicted of offences against children and that it was the department's duty to make sure that he didn't have contact with the children.

"What did he do?" Steph asked the duty officer.

"I'll get his file and ring you back."

"OK."

Steph received a text from John

"Are you OK?" he said.

"I'm fine, xxx," Steph texted back.

It was several weeks since that embarrassing incident with John. He was busy with his programme. He was still seeing Clare but he had said that it wasn't serious.

"Come up for the weekend next week," he texted.

"Ring u tonite," she texted back.

The phone rang, it was the duty officer from Blackpool.

"Violence and sexual offences," was the reply of the duty officer. "He spent five years inside." She gave Steph enough information for her to realise the imminent dangers to the children.

Martin was out of the office, there was only Sarah still in and she was due to go on a visit.

"Is Martin coming back?" said Steph.

"No," Sarah replied.

"Bugger," Steph exclaimed.

"What's up?"

"Looks like we might have an EPO."

Steph knew that to get an Emergency Protection Order at this time of day on a Friday without a manager around would be difficult. They would have to explain to a magistrate why they felt that the risk was so great that the children would have to be removed. Steph knew very little about the mother. The records on the file were very sparse. It was now 3.30pm and the children had gone home.

"Bugger," she said again.

The headteacher of the school was very good; she didn't report things unless she felt that the children were in danger and always worked very cooperatively with social services but, like many headteachers, she had a tendency to report things too late in the day.

Steph rang down to reception to see which managers were still in the office. She found that there weren't any.

"Bugger," she said.

"Look, I'll cancel my meeting," said Sarah.

"Thanks," said Steph. She knew that she couldn't do this one alone.

"So what happened in the end?" said John.

"We had to ring headquarters and Martin came back."

"Blackpool gave enough information to show the high level of risk and, bearing in mind that the mother hadn't worked very cooperatively with us, we knew that she couldn't be trusted to make sure that he was out of the house."

"And so where are the children now?"

"They went to their paternal granny's house, the mum of the guy who is in prison, but it's not ideal. So how's the filming going?"

"Nearly finished. Are you coming up here? It would be a change for you, Steph, and I haven't seen you for ages."

"OK, I've got Friday off so I could catch a train on Thursday night. How's Clare?"

"She's fine, great. Better go, I can smell something burning in the kitchen."

Steph put the phone down. She could imagine the burning smell. John had always been good at starting cooking and then getting into a long telephone conversation with someone. He didn't usually burn things though and she wondered whether this was just an excuse to get off the phone. Their relationship had changed since that night when she had thrown herself at him. She had just felt so needy she had wanted to be cuddled, to be loved like Alan had loved her.

She thought of the three children staying with their granny; she didn't look the sort who would give them many cuddles. They had been such adorable children and Steph thought what fun she could have had with them if she had been their mum.

She hugged her tummy and longed for the child that she had lost. She tried hard not to cry too much these days as she knew how much it upset her mum and dad. She was so lucky to have such fabulous parents. Since Alan had died his parents had little to do with her. Her dad said that it was just that they were finding it hard dealing with their own grief. Steph understood but it hurt so much.

Her parents had gone to a concert that had been booked for ages. They had asked her if she would be OK and she had reassured them that she would but now the tears flooded down her cheeks. She wasn't OK, she was so miserable.

Chapter Five

"Bloody paperwork," screamed Sarah. "What is expected of us is just so unreasonable."

"Team meeting," announced Martin.

The room hadn't been booked and so the team members squeezed into Martin's office.

"Who wants to chair?" said Martin.

"I will," said Steph.

She was feeling more positive today and more in control of her caseload. She had the next day off and was looking forward to going to Manchester to see John.

"So how is everyone feeling?" she said.

Different team members expressed their views. They came to Sarah and she said that she just felt that she was drowning under the ridiculous amount of paperwork.

"Sometimes I want to scream," she said. "I've taken two kids into care this week and all the paperwork is so ludicrous and repetitive."

Tony, a new member of the team, sympathised. He said that he felt uncomfortable because he was undertaking his induction and could see the pressure on team members.

"You'll soon be in the same boat," said Luke.

Steph shared out the mound of notices and circulars. Sarah burst out laughing.

"Martin, where have you been hiding this one?" she said. "It's months past the closing date." She was referring to a course in London. "And look at the price," she giggled. "Oh, we can just see the authority paying £300 plus VAT, and the travel and accommodation." She laughed sarcastically.

Steph could feel the stress in the air. It was as thick as a hard cheese.

Martin tried his best to alleviate pressure but the quantity of work was just so huge. They got to the allocation of cases and yet again Sarah burst into what seemed to Steph like hysterical laughter.

"Why are we doing this?" Sarah exclaimed.

Those words resounded in Steph's head as she got on the train to Manchester. She didn't have to be a social worker but she knew that there was already too much passing the buck.

She had felt so vulnerable when Alan had died but now, most of the time, she found that she had a survival instinct which she never knew that she had. She just had to survive. John had told her that one day she would be happy again but for now it was just surviving.

She worked with people who had survived for years. She would have liked to wave a magic wand to make them all happy but she knew that she couldn't.

She had recently become restless both at home and in her job and had wondered whether she should take up John's offer to go and live in Manchester. She loved her parents dearly but she was too old to still be living with them. It would have been different if she had always lived there but she had left ages ago. Her life with Steve now felt like a distant memory.

The train made good progress and she texted John to say that they had just passed Stoke. She wondered what it would be like to work in Stoke. It had once been part of Staffordshire but was now a unitary authority. She had a friend who had been brought up there and had told her about Staffordshire oatcakes. She said that they were a bit like pancakes. She felt hungry and realised that she had missed lunch without even knowing.

There was an announcement over the tannoy to say that they were approaching Manchester Piccadilly. Steph suddenly felt an excitement which seemed new. She was going to see John and the idea of seeing him again just sent tingles through her body.

John had planned to leave at ten past but had received a call from the studio to say could he go in as they were having a problem with one of the scenes. He said that he would be there in an hour. That would give him enough time to collect Steph. He didn't know whether she would want to come with him but he would ask her.

He couldn't find the car keys and started to panic. He remembered that he had put them in his desk and, sure enough, they were there.

Steph got off the train and looked for John but there was no sign of him. For a second she panicked but breathed deeply knowing that he had probably just got caught up in the traffic. She went to the magazine stand and bought herself a Woman's Own. One of the articles on the front page caught her eye. "How I survived," it read. Steph wondered what the woman smiling back at her had survived. She caught a glimpse of her own face in the glass surrounding the stall and realised that she looked so glum. She forced a smile and at that precise moment a man looked directly at her and, thinking that she was smiling at him, smiled back at her. It made her feel warm inside. She smiled at another couple of people and they too smiled back.

The man that had first smiled at her hovered around and then came towards her.

"Are you OK?" he said.

"Yes, I'm just waiting for a friend, he must have got caught up in traffic."

"That's OK then," he replied and moved away from Steph. He continued to gaze at her. She tried to look away but she found herself pulled to his eyes. Eyes that seemed to sparkle with life.

"Look," he said, "I know this is crazy, but what's your name? It's just you remind me of someone I used to know, that's all. I know that this sounds like an awful pick-up line but you just seem so familiar."

"It's Steph," she said, "and I have to go."

Steph had spied John coming towards her.

"Hi John," said the stranger.

"Hi Mike, where are you off to?"

14

"London," he replied.

"You know each other?" said Steph.

"Yes. Mike is an executive in the TV company and will be promoting my drama."

"What a small world," said Mike.

"Are you John's girlfriend?"

"No just a good friend, that's all."

Steph found herself attracted to Mike. He was the first man who she had even bothered to look at for months.

"He's married with two kids," said John as they walked towards the car.

"He's gorgeous," said Steph.

"Might be, but it'll be playing with fire," said John, who suddenly felt a pang of jealousy.

Chapter Six

Steph had never been to a TV studio before. It all seemed rather chaotic but John reassured her on the way home that it would all turn out fine.

"How do you know?" she said. "I thought that you were a hack."

"Well, you don't know everything about me," John said with a sparkle in his eye. "I actually started with TV work but then transferred to journalism."

"Why?" said Steph.

"I think that my prof. thought that I would be better at it and he had a lot of contacts."

"But I thought you said that he wanted you to go to Manchester."

"He did, but he knew people in London as well."

John's mobile rang and he answered it.

"Yes, she's here … so you are coming over then … about eight, we'll eat out … oh wherever you like. Steph likes any kind of food. See you later."

"That was Clare, you don't mind her coming over do you?"

"Of course not, she's bound to want to suss me out."

Steph had a pang of jealousy. She would have preferred John on her own but she couldn't intrude into his life.

They left the studio and popped to Tesco to do some shopping.

"Don't tell me you've run out of bog roll," she said.

"Steph, you know me, I am a useless shopper."

They giggled together and linked arms along the road. Suddenly John started running and pulled Steph along with him. He laughed as she lost her balance but he caught her and for a few seconds felt captivated by her eyes. She too felt this strange trance-like effect and then John's mobile played its familiar tune.

"Yes, I'll get some toothpaste see you later."

"Where were we?" John said.

"You were trying to drag me along the street and then I got caught in a trance until your mobile rang," Steph said.

"I felt just the same," John replied.

"Must have been witches flying by," Steph giggled.

"'Spose so," said John.

They got in the car and started on the journey to John's house when he suddenly turned around.

"What are you doing?" Steph exclaimed.

"I forgot the toothpaste."

Steph giggled.

"You'd forget the baby," she said.

John heard the word baby and soon he felt broody again. Why did Steph have to mention babies? He knew that Clare wasn't interested in kids and he had given up on the idea of ever being with Steph.

The toothpaste was near to the baby things and John found himself looking at the different variety of nappies.

"Can I help you?" said a young woman near to him. "Has your wife sent you for a special brand?"

"I don't have a wife," John blurted out, feeling rather stupid.

"Oh, so you are a single dad."

John felt himself getting trapped. If he said that he wasn't she might think that he was some kind of pervert. If he said that he was that would be a complete lie which he could never get himself out of. Suddenly Steph appeared and said, "Oh darling, it's about time you knew what type Tommy wears."

The young woman frowned and went away.

"I just told her that I didn't have a wife," John said.

"Oh," Steph giggled. She poked John in the ribs.

"We better take this one," Steph said, picking up a boys' middle size.

They came into the house giggling. Clare was in the kitchen making herself a coffee.

"Sounds like you two have been having some fun."

Clare looked stony-faced as Steph retold the story of the nappies.

"Oh come on Clare, lighten up," said John.

"I can't see what's funny, that's all."

During the evening both Steph and John found themselves in fits of giggles. They tried to include Clare but she just didn't seem to see what was funny.

"I think I'll go home," said Clare as she got to the house.

"Are you sure?" said John. "Why don't you stay over?"

"Because two's company and three's a crowd," said Clare.

"It's OK, I'll go to bed and leave you to it," said Steph feeling rather embarrassed.

"No, I'll go and perhaps see you in the week, John."

"Yes, I'm sure," he said as he kissed her on the cheek.

John giggled. "We were so naughty, but she is so serious. She just can't be playful like you; you know Steph, it's just great having you here."

"Its great being here, but I don't want to intrude into your love life."

"You're not. Do you ever see David and Ian?" said John.

"Oh, from time to time."

"Fancy some fizz pop?"

"Yep."

"I'll pop to the offy and get some."

"Can I have a bath?"

"Of course, you can borrow my dressing gown if you like."

"Thanks."

Steph lay back in the warm water and found herself drifting off. She felt very at home in John's house. She recognised the towels that he had when he lived in her house. He still had the broken sponge shaped like a duck whose head had got pulled off one night when they had a play fight. She remembered that it was just a few days before she had met Alan in the supermarket. That all seemed such a long time ago.

She felt that she had always known John and she heard the latch on the door as he returned and the familiar sound of his voice as he shouted his return, but another voice also shouted along with his. It was Clare, she had obviously come back. She couldn't trust Steph and John to be alone together and Steph knew exactly why.

Chapter Seven

"Can you cover my duty for me please, Steph? I'll do one for you," said Luke.

"OK but you'll have to do one in return because I've got to get that court report done."

Steph was jotting down some notes from a previous call when the phone rang.

"Hello, this is Steph, can I help you?" Steph said.

"This is Brian Lewis from the Daily Echo. We'd like to know Social Services' view on the sex offender living at number 28 Gregory Street."

"I'll have to pass you on to our headquarters," said Steph.

"I've tried them but there is no one there."

"Well, I really can't comment," said Steph, "I know nothing about the man you are talking about."

"Aren't you the social worker whose husband was murdered a while back?" he said.

Steph just froze and put the phone down.

"What's the matter?" said Sarah as she saw Steph looking into thin air. Steph found that she couldn't speak.

"Steph, I'm worried about you, are you alright?"

Steph sat motionless.

Sarah went to get Martin from his office. Martin put his arms around Steph and she clung to him and cried. She told Martin about the journalist and Martin fumed. "The little shit," he said. "And to think that your best friend is a journalist. You should get him on to him. Let's ring John now. Give me his phone number."

Steph silently wrote down John's number and listened as Martin recounted to John what had happened.

The newspaper the next day covered the story of the social worker who defended the pervert.

"I didn't say any of that," Steph screamed. "He has made it all up, I told him that I didn't even know who this guy was. It was just ... when he said about Alan that I put the phone down."

"Everyone understands Steph, the guy should never have got past reception, he was just too clever, that's all."

The rest of the week was a hard slog and all Steph's service users appeared to be more dependent on her than usual. She was so glad when it was time to go home on the Friday.

Steph entered the house and her mum said that there was a guy sitting in the living room.

"He said that he had met you briefly and that he was a friend of John's ... he's a very good looking, charming man," she remarked, "and well turned out too."

Steph went into the living room and there, chatting to her dad, was Mike, the man that she had met at Piccadilly station while she was waiting for John.

"I was passing," said Mike, "and so I thought I'd just pop in to say hello." Steph's dad said that he was popping out and that it was a pleasure meeting him and winked at Steph in a knowing way.

"Just passing?" said Steph. "How can you be just passing when you live in Manchester?"

"OK, I lied, I just wanted to see you again, that's all."

"And what does your wife think about you popping all the way to Birmingham to see a woman that you just happened to bump into at Manchester Piccadilly station?"

"She wouldn't care, she hates my guts and won't let me see the kids."

"Oh yes? I've heard that kind of story before. No, go Mike, I just can't get tangled up with you, life has been too difficult for me and I just couldn't cope. Besides how did you know where I lived?"

"OK" he said. "It's a shame though, I think that we would get on great together." Steph shut the door and wondered who would be the next man who would try and take advantage of her. Mike had not even told her how he got her address

"He did what?" said John, as Steph told him how Mike had just turned up at the house. How he knew where she lived was a mystery. "His wife is besotted with him; he told you complete lies. I can't understand how he thought that he would get away with it." He went on "We've finished filming, it's all with editing now; you should see some publicity about it in a couple of months. I'm writing more for the Daily Feature, Steph. They want to give me a social affairs column. I was thinking of calling it 'Patience and Courage', what do you think?"

"That's the name I wanted for the TV prog but I suppose you'll be able to explain it more in a column. Will it be PC for short?" she joked.

John squirmed, not really saying anything.

"Did you know that Lucy and Tom are getting married?"

"When?"

"Midsummer's Day."

"What a romantic time to get married," John exclaimed "I think if I ever got married again I'd like to get married on Midsummer's Day … got to go, Clare has just arrived."

Steph still enjoyed her chats with John although she was aware that Clare wasn't happy with their relationship; but then she couldn't claim that there wasn't something for her to be unhappy about. She had made overtures to John but he had made it plain that he was no longer interested in her that way, so she would have to accept the relationship the way it was.

John opened the door to Clare. She was a beautiful woman but she had none of the inner beauty that Steph had. He could listen to Steph for hours but regularly he would get bored with Clare droning on. But she was company and that's what he most wanted at the moment.

He had told Steph that there was no chance romantically between them and had nearly convinced himself that this was the case but there was just something about her.

Chapter Eight

"Welcome, Mark, to the team," said Martin.

"Its good to be here," said Mark.

Mark was very dark skinned, tall and distinctive rather than good looking. He had been with the team for three days.

"Its good to have another permanent, full-time member of staff," said Martin. "We've had so many different agency workers."

"Well, you've had one for some time," said Nancy. "You know that I'd really like to be permanent but I need to be off with the kids in the summer. It is just too difficult and too expensive to pay for childcare during the summer holidays. If Social Services departments were a bit more flexible then I could be permanent."

"I know," said Martin.

They discussed the latest pressures on the team and the incident with the journalist who managed to get through reception.

"We are all so introverted," Steph said. "We should be proud of a lot of what we do."

She told the team about John's column.

"I'll look forward to reading it," said Martin, "but why is it to be called 'Patience and Courage'?"

"Because journalists and the media need to be a bit more patient with us. They take ages to make programmes but we are supposed to protect children and sort out lives in an instant. The courage is us; we need to start realising that the public might actually be interested in what we do."

They talked at length about the stigma surrounding a lot of social work.

"But we shouldn't reinforce it," said Steph.

"You are such an idealist," said Luke. "We are so powerless, Steph."

"So that's why we need to become more courageous."

After the team meeting Mark came and sat near to Steph. He said that he agreed a great deal with what she had said. He had moved to Birmingham two years ago from London with his girlfriend and had worked through an agency. Soon after they arrived she went off with a work colleague. As a reaction, he decided just to date anyone he could find but soon realised that none of them were right for him. He was now computer dating and had met a few nice women but not the right one yet. He also liked living in Birmingham and so he decided to stay and part of the reason for getting a permanent job was so that he could get a mortgage to buy a house.

Steph told him her own story, about Steve and Alan.

"It must have been awful," he said.

"It was, and it's the anniversary of Alan's death next week."

Steph thought no more of the chat that she had with Mark until Lucy brought it up.

"So you've had a long chat with the new guy in your team?"

"How did you know?"

"He was talking about different team members and mentioned you."

Lucy was working in the Family Placement team and so was in regular contact with Steph's team when they rang wanting placements for children, some of whom were suddenly at risk. She had moaned to Steph that it was supposed to be planned work but that it often wasn't.

They chatted about Mark and then went on to the wedding.

"Do you want me to invite John or not?"

"It's up to you Lucy."

"I will then," she said.

"Look John, we have been together a while now; I wondered whether it is the right time for me to move in and see how we get on as a real couple," Clare said.

"I'm not sure," said John.

But what he really thought was that it wasn't what he wanted at all.

"Steph, I really don't want her to move in, she will drive me mad."

"So she's alright for a bit of how's your father but not as a proper partner; that's what you are saying, is it?"

"You make it sound so seedy."

"Well it is, isn't it?"

"Tell me about the new bloke in the team then? Do you fancy him?"

Steph told John about Mark. She did fancy him a little but she wasn't going to tell John, it kind of didn't feel quite right.

She often felt like this these days as she began to realize that she could fancy men again but no longer was it disloyalty to Alan because she knew that Alan would never be coming back. No, it was that feeling towards John; and yet he had made it plain that they would never be more than friends.

John was to come and stay with her family the night before Lucy's wedding and the night of the wedding. He had not stayed there for ages and so it seemed a little odd.

Chapter Nine

"You need to go out on a twosome on this one," said Martin. "Take Mark with you."

Mark was coming to the end of his induction period and had taken on a few cases but he wasn't as busy as the rest of the team.

"Do you want to drive or me?" Steph said as she put her diary and notepad into her bag.

"I'll drive and you can navigate," Mark said.

"You're bound to get lost then," Luke commented, looking up from his recording.

Steph stuck her tongue out at him and pulled a funny face.

She felt a lot happier these days, the shadows of doom and gloom were lifting and she no longer felt guilty about laughing and enjoying herself. All the team had noticed and had commented how lovely it was to have the old Steph back.

Steph liked Mark; he was easy to talk to and didn't come on to her at all. He also seemed to be good at his job and hadn't become cynical like so many social workers had. He didn't like the over-bureaucratic system but instead of moaning he did something about it. He had started a website so that social workers and journalists could share their experiences. It was called scampweb.com, which stood for social care and media people. He said that he had tried to get the words social work into the initials but all the words seemed so negative.

Steph had told Mark about John and he had said that he would like to meet him sometime.

As they drove to the Carters' house Steph found herself distracted by Mark. "Are you OK?" said Mark as he looked in the mirror.

He was a careful driver.

"I'm fine, it's just that I know that Ian Carter can be rather abusive when he has had a drink and Linda sounded pretty desperate."

"Are the police coming too?"

"Yes, they may have to do an PPO as the quickest way to get the kids out of there if Linda doesn't agree to them going, because Ian won't."

"Has this happened before?"

"Yes."

They discussed the ins and outs of the case. Linda had left Ian several times when he had had his violent outbursts but then he would get off the drink, get himself a job and do all the things required of him and then Linda would go back with the kids. Linda's mum had died recently and none of her brothers or sisters were willing to have the kids because of Ian. Ian's brothers were worse than him so this put Social Services in a difficult position with five kids to house.

Besides all of this, the kids were all really nice, which social workers found strange. It was as if they switched off during these crises. They all loved their mum and dad. Steph knew that Ian loved Linda and the kids but he could never completely kick the drink habit.

Some social workers in the past had tried to get the kids permanently taken into care but they would always say that they wanted to go back home or would run back home from their placements.

The twins were the oldest and at fourteen were two delightful girls. Emma and Emily would take charge of the other children and would do tasks that not many other kids of their age would have to do.

Steph had one more look at Mark as they arrived at the house. He had the most wonderful clear, smooth skin and his shaved head seemed just as smooth.

The police had already arrived. Three of the children and Linda were out in the street being comforted by a neighbour. Steph quickly ascertained from the police that Ian had locked himself in the bathroom with the baby and one of the twins.

She rang the office to tell Martin what was happening.

"Oh shit," he said, "he must really have blown it this time."

The police knew that all the kids were on the Child Protection register. It was Sarah's family but she was on a course in Leicester today and Steph, as the duty officer, had to take charge.

"He might have a gun," Steph told the Inspector. "It has been rumoured for some time; that's why we all visit the family in twos."

The Inspector was the same guy who had found Alan and Paul; he remembered Steph. "Are you OK with this?" he said.

"You mean because of Alan and Paul? Yes, Steve, I am."

And she knew that she was. The cloud was finally lifted and she could move on.

A few minutes later there was a commotion and the twin and baby came out of the house. Immediately afterwards there was the sound of a gunshot and then silence.

By now armed police had arrived on the scene. The whole street remained silent for a few seconds and then Steph heard the Inspector order the armed police to enter the house.

Chapter Ten

It was ten o'clock by the time that Mark and Steph left Linda and the children. The police had shut off the house, so Linda and the children went to stay with her elder sister. Now that the family knew that the threat of Ian had disappeared they were willing to help her out.

"A good riddance," Elaine had said to Steph when Linda was out of earshot.

Steph didn't comment. She knew that it would make life easier for Sarah when she returned to support Linda but Steph felt sad that Ian had been driven to such extremes by drink.

"Fancy a drink?" Mark said.

"OK," said Steph, but as she drank her diet coke she looked around the pub and wondered how many other men would turn out like Ian.

"I don't suppose this is a good time but, well, Steph, I like you and, well, I just wondered if you'd come on a date with me," said Mark.

Steph looked at Mark and didn't reply.

"I shouldn't have asked," he said, "not today with all the memories of your own experience."

"No, it's OK Mark, yes I'd love to go out with you but I'm rather tired and so if you can just drop me off at the office to get my car, we can arrange it tomorrow if we are in at the same time."

"Yes, that would be good."

They drove silently back to the office and then back to there seperate homes.

Steph walked in the front door and found Dad on the phone. "It's Lucy for you."

Steph hung her coat up in the hall and dumped her bag. She took the phone up to her room and lay on the bed.

"So when is this date?" Lucy said.

"We haven't fixed it yet."

"Does that mean that I'll have to invite the awful Clare to my wedding?"

"Why?"

"Well, if you bring Mark, John will be all alone."

"I haven't even had a first date yet," Steph laughed.

Steph arrived at work and Martin asked her to come straight away into the office.

"Are you OK?" he said.

"Yes, I'm fine Martin. I would tell you if I wasn't."

"It just must have brought back memories, that's all."

"In a way it sorted things forever," Steph said and left Martin to think on this.

"So are we still on for that date?" said Mark.

"Yes," said Steph as she copied her LAC documents.

"What about Saturday?"

"Yes that's fine."

Steph didn't see Mark for the rest of the day. Sarah thanked her for what she had done the day before and checked too that she was OK.

"I'm fine," she said, and she was. She was ready to go on a date with Mark.

She was ready to fall in love again and she texted John to tell him about yesterday and the date.

That evening John rang Steph. He wanted her advice on how to get rid of Clare. He knew that there was just no future with her.

He listened to Steph retelling the horrific events of the day. She had asked John how he would have reported it and laughed at his answer. And he knew that, frankly, he was jealous; he loved Steph and yet his pride wouldn't let him tell her in case, yet again, he got rejected. So he put on a good encouraging act and said that if he went to the wedding on his own that perhaps he would find a nice woman amongst the guests.

Steph said that she felt that he would and for an instant felt those pangs that she had once felt for John. But now she had a new adventure with a new man and she was going to enjoy going out with Mark. He was an interesting, warm man and that was more than enough for her now.

Chapter Eleven

Everyone was rather manic at the team meeting. It had been a crazy week and the whole team felt that they had to chill out.

"You must think that we are all mad," said Steph to Mark after the meeting.

"No, very human," he replied, looking at Steph in an endearing way. "I'm really looking forward to Saturday," he said.

"Me too," Steph replied as she left the office for her next visit.

It was one she liked. It was a bit of a journey, as it was a child who was fostered and the nearest appropriate foster parents were over an hour's drive away. It was also a more expensive placement as the foster parents were employed by a private fostering agency. This grated a bit with Steph as she knew that there were local people who would take on this task if only the local authority allowances were a bit more. The team were always complaining, as most social workers did, about this discrepancy, but these carers were good and the lad that they had staying with them had been in so many placements that it was good to see him settled. He was now thirteen and had been with them for about eighteen months. To start with it was a bit tricky but now the placement was working well and it was hoped that he would stay there until he was eighteen.

At times Steph had got angry thinking of Paul, as this lad's situation was very similar to Paul's, but when Martin queried her having the case she was insistent that it really was appropriate. She arrived at the house about ten minutes later than she had planned.

"You are looking very happy," said Shirley, the foster mum.

"Yes, I am a lot happier these days. How is Dean?"

"He's fine and doing well at school. We think that he even has a bit of a crush on a girl at school."

"Is that good, or bad?"

"Knowing the girl's family, it's good."

The door banged and Dean came in the living room.

"Hiya, Steph," he said, with a big grin all over his face.

Steph always liked her visits, as it seemed such a happy household. Shirley had fostered loads of kids. She used to foster through the local authority. She had been a single parent for years bringing up three kids of her own but three years ago she had met Pete and life had changed. Pete was a single man who had never really had a long-term relationship and at the age of forty-eight was still living at home with his parents.

When he moved in with Shirley two years ago and they married soon after, the local authority had to check him out to make sure that he had no previous records of abuse against children. Some social workers were suspicious because he was still living at home but he was a lovely man who adored Shirley and her children. Shirley had decided to change to a private agency because of the attitude towards Pete.

Pete had told Steph on one of her visits about a friend of his, who was ten years younger than him, who was still living with his parents and was a friendly helpful person. Pete said that he was a lovely man who just liked to help wherever he could. He worked as a painter and decorator. At one household where he did some work, the mother of four girls was disabled and the father was in the forces. He had got to know the family and had become good friends to all of them. When the father was away, if they needed help they would turn to him but unfortunately this all backfired. Not in the way that you would imagine with him falling for the mum. He had a girlfriend of his own. Unfortunately, one of the daughters accused him of interfering with her which led to him being arrested and spending a long time at the police station. They took all his computer equipment away. They never found anything but it made him permanently wary and for a time he wasn't allowed to go to Pete and Shirley's house. In the end Shirley contacted her MP and he agreed that he was no risk to any kids. The daughter who accused him also accused her father, which lead to a major investigation as he was a colonel in the army.

Pete had talked to Steph about how mad the world had become and Steph agreed. The team had discussed the issues and half felt that he was guilty whereas the other half believed that the girl's mental state and watching too much television had caused her behaviour. The army paid for an expert psychiatrist to quiz her father and he was found to be completely innocent and a caring father and husband. But Pete said that his friend still wouldn't visit his and Shirley's house if the girls were there on their own.

"What do you think, John?" Steph had said at the time.

"It's a knee jerk reaction" John replied. "It makes a great story."

"That's cruel," said Steph.

"No, I've never written one like that myself but I have known journalists that have."

"And what do they think?"

"Not sure some of them do, they just see cash."

"But surely there are others that have a conscience?"

"Of course, many, if not most."

Steph remembered this conversation and felt for Pete's friend.

"So how's things Dean? Have you seen your mum?"

"Yes, I saw her at the weekend, but Steph, her new guy is such a pillock."

"Oh dear, that doesn't sound good, I'll have to go and visit her. Is he living there?"

"Not officially, but I think that he's there a lot of the time."

"So what do Charlene and Jenny think of him?"

"Not much, they say that he gets drunk and swears at Mum."

"Look Dean, I'll check it out for you, you needn't worry. We can get you to meet with mum and the girls away from the house for now."

Dean had previously run away from placements back home to protect his mum as she always seem to land herself with a violent partner. The family had been known to social services since Dean was a baby and all of the children at times had been fostered. It was agreed that Dean would never return to his mum and a care order had been taken out but his sisters had been returned home. He missed them desperately. It was felt that Charlene, who was now twelve, would probably eventually need to be looked after on a permanent basis too.

Cases like these caused so much distress to the team as they knew that all they could do was try to prevent any serious physical harm happening to the children. The long-term psychological effects could only be guessed.

Programmes such as Trisha often discussed the long-term effects and blamed social workers for not doing more but what could they do?

Steph reassured Dean but as she left to battle the rush-hour traffic home she wondered whether she would return to work the next day to find a message from Shirley and the police to say that Dean had absconded. How could she ever feel the love that Dean felt for his mum?

Chapter Twelve

"Oh I'm glad that week's over," said Steph as she signed out.

It had been a long, emotional week. Fortunately Dean hadn't absconded. He had talked to his mum and she was coming to visit him on Sunday at the foster carers', with his sisters.

Steph went out into the cool air and breathed it in deeply. She thought of her date with Mark the next day and suddenly felt excited.

"Bye," she said as she passed George having his last fag before he headed home.

"Bye, have a good weekend Steph," he replied.

"You too," Steph acknowledged.

Steph arrived home completely forgetting that her Aunt Sheila and Uncle Stan were coming for the weekend.

"And how's our little girl then?" said Uncle Stan.

He always had a joke with her and would always get scolded by her aunt for speaking to her in such a way.

Aunt Sheila was her mum's older sister and usually came to stay for a couple of weekends a year and would go for a fortnight's holiday with her parents during the summer. They had an only child, Harry, who was about eighteen months older than Steph. The two families had often hoped that Steph and Harry might get together. He was a clever man who had a PhD in English Literature and was a Senior Lecturer but Steph had always found him rather arrogant and opinionated.

"Oh, Harry has come too," Steph's mum whispered. "He kind of invited himself, but we haven't seen him for ages; you will try to get on with him, won't you?"

"When are they going home?" Steph asked.

"I'm not sure, Sunday night or Monday morning."

"Hello Steph, I haven't seen you for years," Harry said as he came into the kitchen. "I just wondered whether you needed any help."

Steph looked at this good looking man and wondered if it was the same man that she remembered.

"You look surprised," Harry said.

"It's…"

"You think that I've changed?"

Steph didn't say a word.

That night Steph's mum had made an extra special effort with tea. Her sister, although nice, was a bit of a snob and so Mum had made sure that everything was in its place.

Steph had brought some work home and so shut herself away before tea to catch up.

"You won't be long, will you?" said Mum. "I thought we'd all go out to a nice country pub afterwards."

"OK, Mum, just relax, she's only your sister."

Steph concentrated on her report and just got it completed as Harry knocked on her door and told her that tea would be ready in ten minutes.

Steph logged on to the internet and emailed the report to the office. She then looked at the three emails waiting for her. There were also two in the bulk and so Steph looked at them first. They were the usual junk mail, which she immediately deleted.

32

There was an email from Lucy reminding her of the details for her hen party next week, one from John, which looked rather long and one for which she didn't recognise the sender. She decided to look at the mysterious one first. She realised that it was from John's work colleague who she had briefly met at the station. It read:

I know that John has told you that I am married with children but he doesn't know my whole story. You see, Steph, I married very young to the girl next door and for seven years we were very happy. We were married for five years and then had Katy our first daughter. Two years later we had Mandy our second daughter. After Mandy was born my wife went off sex and I, disgracefully, had an affair. It lasted for about eight months and then I stopped it. I loved my wife and I didn't know whether to tell her or not. I decided not to tell her but the woman I had an affair with wouldn't accept that it was over and she rang my wife.

My wife was heartbroken and one day, when I was at work, took an overdose. My children were both very small at the time and one of them was screaming so much that a neighbour came around. The doctors told me that if she hadn't come round that my wife would have probably died.

I felt so guilty and regretted what I had done. The woman continued to pester me and my wife insisted that I was still having an affair. I told her that I wasn't but she wouldn't believe me and would regularly try to kill herself.

This has been going on now for the past fifteen years. My youngest will soon be sixteen and doesn't want a party because of it.

I just wanted you to know, Steph, that's all.

I saw you at the station that day and just felt something I hadn't felt for so long. Sorry for bothering you.

Mike.

"Tea's ready," shouted Dad up the stairs.

Steph shut the laptop down and unplugged the cables.

She went downstairs and remembered that she hadn't read John's email. She would read it later. She wondered why Mike had sent her an email and also how he knew her email address. Suddenly life seemed to be complicated again. She had a date with Mark tomorrow, gazed across at her cousin, who seemed a changed man, wondered about the mysterious Mike and still felt those feelings when she thought of her John and was so glad to hear that he was at last going to dump the awful Clare.

Chapter Thirteen

The date with Mark was nice. She really enjoyed his company, he was such a sweet man but she was glad to get home.

"I'd like to do it again," Mark said as he kissed Steph.

"Yes, that would be nice," said Steph.

"We'll fix something from work; see you on Monday, bye."

Mark stood for a minute and then he hugged and kissed Steph once more before he walked towards his car.

"Did you have a nice time?" said Dad. "Why didn't you invite him in?"

"Too many people around, Dad."

"Yes I suppose so, but you're seeing him again, are you?"

"Oh yes, he's a nice guy."

"Oh, John rang by the way, he was worried about you."

"Why?"

"He said that he hadn't heard from you and had asked some specific questions in his email."

"Oh," Steph remembered that she had forgotten to read John's email so she went into the study and switched on the computer. Harry came strolling in.

"You were back early; I thought that we might not see you until tomorrow, said Harry." He winked at Steph and she cringed, thinking that perhaps she was right that he was still the old Harry that she knew. But then the night before he had seemed so different, so genuine.

She read the email from John and realised why he was worried about her.

"I'll see you later," said Steph as she headed towards her bedroom. She didn't want to talk to John in front of Harry.

"I'm sorry, John, I forgot to read your email."

"Won't bother again," he said trying to sulk.

He had asked Steph all about details for the wedding and so wasn't really worried but needed to make sure that she rang him. Sometimes these days he wouldn't hear from her for several days. He missed hearing her chattery voice or even solemn tones.

Steph told John about the email from Mike.

"I wondered how he got my email."

"I kind of gave it to him," said John in a guilty tone. "But I didn't give him your address."

"Why did you do that?"

"We got into a conversation about social workers and how little most of the media knew about what you did and somehow I just gave him your email. It was as a contact in case he ever needed some input from a social worker. It wasn't intended..." John hesitated as he said this. "I never dreamt..."

"Don't worry, there's no harm done."

John suddenly felt a pang of jealousy. What was he doing pushing Steph into the arms of someone like Mike? He had fed her the sob story and she seemed to believe it.

"You won't meet with him, will you Steph?"

"I doubt it," she replied.

But she was too hesitant for John's liking. What had he done? Was he about to lead Steph down another path of gloom?

Steph shut her bedroom door as she went downstairs to make a drink. John felt concerned for her. He was very wary of her having anything to do with Mike.

Now that Clare was no longer in John's life he seemed not to be interested in anyone. She knew that it was early days. He had certainly changed from the man that she first knew. He was still just as good looking with a nice body but his soul was different.

She thought about Lucy's imminent wedding and that John would be there and she smiled thinking of the different times that she and John had together when they lived under the same roof. She cringed a little when she thought of the overtures that she had made to him when she was rather drunk. Yes, John was a dear friend who was always there for her but was that enough?

"Are you making me a cuppa?" said Harry as he came into the kitchen.

"What do you want?"

"You," said Harry as he grabbed hold of Steph and tried to kiss her. She pulled away, but he was so strong.

"You know you want it," Harry said, "so why not just chill out and enjoy yourself. That Mark bloke isn't right for you. Besides, do you really want to have a load of smelly niggers?"

Steph couldn't believe this. She tried to pull away but he just held her more firmly. She wanted to scream but nothing would come out.

Chapter Fourteen

The train seemed to take ages getting to Manchester. Steph thought of the night before and what might have happened if her father hadn't come down for a drink.

Harry had said he was sorry but that wasn't the point. Steph had felt so frightened and even though it was after midnight she had thought nothing of ringing John, the dearest friend that she had ever had. She had loved Alan but she couldn't talk to Alan about anything and everything as she could with John.

Lucy's wedding was in just a few days and John said that he would drive Steph back and stay an extra few days. She had rung Martin at home just before she left and he had said that it was OK for her not to come into work until Wednesday. It was now Sunday, so that would give her two days to potter around Manchester.

The train seemed to stop everywhere.

She thought of her mum's reaction.

"Do you have to go so suddenly?"

"Yes, Mum, he gets on my nerves."

She didn't want to tell her mum that he had come on so strong to her that she feared for her safety. She knew that if Steve had been around he would have socked him one. Alan would probably have tried to talk out the situation and John would just have grabbed Steph away.

She felt weak and vulnerable. In her work she had never put herself at this level of risk. Did she really want him to overpower and control her? She feared that this might be partly true. Perhaps she really wanted to be submissive and her enduring strength was just one big sham. She had been the flirtatious woman who, if she worked at it hard enough, could get any man that she really wanted. She had flirted with Harry. She had realised that the man who used to repulse her was, in fact, rather attractive, or was he? Was she just desperate to surround herself with men to distract herself from the hollow pain that she felt without Alan.

The train pulled into Manchester Piccadilly and there, smiling at her, was the consistent man in her life. Her dear John who she relied on so much for her sanity. The man who, before he met her, could get any woman that he wanted and now seemed to have lost his touch. He was so shocked when she rang. He had had an early night and spoke in a sleepy voice but he was suddenly wide awake when she told him about Harry.

"You must get a train to Manchester first thing in the morning," he had said, but she had too much to do so arrived in Manchester around 6pm.

She lifted her bag and placed herself in the queue to get off the train. The queue moved slowly and Steph began to panic that she wouldn't get off the train. "Breath deeply," she thought. She did and she got control again. She reached the doorway, stepped down out of the train and walked towards John. He was standing near to the exit sign. He saw her, came swiftly towards her and she found herself wrapped in his arms. He kissed her gently on the cheek.

A few seconds later, they walked out of the exit, he carrying her suitcase in one hand and holding her hand with the other.

"Steph, I thought it was you on the train, what are you doing here?" said a woman who approached her. "And who is this dishy man. I was so sorry to hear about Alan and Paul. It's ages since I've seen you."

Steph was desperately trying to remember who this woman was and then suddenly it came to her. She had been on her social work course and she had met her again on an NSPCC training course a few months before Alan died.

"Sorry, Jean, I didn't recognise you for a minute; this is my friend John who used to live in my house in Birmingham. I am back living with my parents at the moment. John, Jean was on the same social work course as me in Birmingham."

"Look, do you fancy a quick drink for old times' sakes?" said Jean.

Steph looked across at John, who seemed to take a fancy to Jean.

"That's OK by me," said John.

One drink led to another and then Steph found herself back at John's, not for a cosy night for two but feeling a little like a gooseberry amongst the Chinese takeaway.

"I'm gonna leave you two owls, I've had a long day," said Steph.

She snuggled down in bed and fell into a deep sleep.

Chapter Fifteen

Steph went to the studio with John. She found the filming interesting.

"What do you reckon then?" said John.

"Very interesting."

"But is it real?"

"I can't really tell, you'll have to read me part of the script." said Steph.

Mike came walking towards her.

"Hi," he said, "nice to see you again."

"Look, I was wrong," said John later, "his story was right. I was talking to a woman who had known him for years. I suppose I was just jealous, that's all."

"You, jealous!" said Steph. "Why on earth should you be jealous?"

The phone rang and so Steph never got her answer. It was Jean and she was inviting herself over again.

"When is she coming?" said Steph in a rather irritated tone.

"In about half an hour, and you are wrong, nothing happened last night. In fact, we were talking shop. That is your shop. She was telling me some very interesting stories about some of the people she was currently working with and I invited her back as I thought that perhaps I could use some of them as storylines if the pilot is a success."

Steph sat feeling rather disgruntled and was glad when eventually Jean said that she had to go.

"I'll give you a lift home," said John.

"Ok, thanks. Tom will wonder where I have got to; he'll think that we are having an affair, with me coming over two nights in a row."

"Who was Tom, then?" said Steph as John hung up his jacket and took off his shoes.

"A young, rather good looking bloke, who is obviously crazy about her. So you needn't worry, she's no competition for you."

"What do you mean?" said Steph.

"Oh, I'm only joking," John said. "Shall we open a bottle of fizz pop?"

"And cuddle like we used to on the settee?" said Steph.

"I was always just about to get my wicked way with you and then something would happen, wouldn't it, like the phone would ring or Alan would arrive. It wasn't always Alan, was it Steph?" John looked directly into her eyes as he said this. "You did feel something for me at times, didn't you?"

He didn't wait for a reply but just continued talking and this time there was nothing or no one to interrupt the flow.

"You see," said John after a lot of talking, "no one could really live up to you, Steph, and that's been my major problem."

Steph didn't know what to say and was glad when the phone did eventually ring and she didn't have to give any kind of reply. It was a colleague of John's who was ringing concerning the next day's schedule.

Steph kissed John on the head and went upstairs to bed.

She lay in bed and the past swirled through her mind. Yes, she had felt a great deal for John and perhaps she still did. But for some reason or other there was also something or someone that got in the way. She thought that it would be better when he moved away to Manchester, and most of the time it was, but there were those moments when she wished that she still had to moan at him about hanging up his towel in the bathroom or pinching the last bit of her toothpaste. But for some time now she had only had herself to moan at. She thought that it was just not being in the control seat at home any more but it was more than that.

She wondered when she would hear his steps on the stairs. Would he wait until she was fast asleep and she would find him sipping coffee in the kitchen the next morning. She didn't drink it herself but she missed the smell. It was part of John, and those curries that he used to make. It was so long since she had had one. John had said that he would make one while she was there but there had been no time and tomorrow they would leave to go back to Birmingham.

John was to sleep on the settee, which was so far from her room. Was this her last chance? Should she seize the moment?

Chapter Sixteen

It seemed strange going into work. Martin was sympathetic.

"You needed the break," he said.

Steph had left John at home.

"You can help with the arrangements for the wedding," Steph giggled.

"I'm good at lifting things," John replied with a smirk.

Steph smiled to herself as she remembered that smirk. Tomorrow was to be a special day. It was a long time since she had been a bridesmaid, or was she a maid of honour. What exactly are you when you are a widow.

She suddenly came out of her daydream. Her young person who had been missing for over a week had been found by the police and was being taken back to her foster parents. This young woman had affected Steph more than others. She was fifteen years old and had been adopted when she was eight years old after spending most of her eight years in a number of foster families.

Her adoptive parents had coped until she was thirteen years old. She had started sniffing glue and stealing from local shops. Then she started to run away, firstly for a day at a time and then it built up into several days. After a year her parents couldn't cope any more and she was placed in a children's home. It wasn't that her parents didn't love her it was just that her early life was thrust back on her and she couldn't cope. She hated her adoptive parents for not telling her about her birth mum and hated her birth mum for choosing her stepdad instead of her. But it just wasn't that simple.

Steph had worked with her for only a few weeks and in that time she had run every few days from the children's home and when the decision was made to place her with experienced foster carers after a very short time she ran again. No one really knew who she was mixing with but no one could believe that anyone that really cared would let her stay away without getting her to make at least one call.

This time it had been awful and so Steph was surprised that Martin had let her go to stay with John. But he knew that there was really nothing more that she could do. She had given the police all of the information that she knew. She and Clare, the foster carer, had gone through her bedroom looking for clues. She hated doing it. Reading her personal diary was particularly difficult but she had to look for clues.

How unhappy this young woman and her parents were. She remembered how she felt losing Alan and Paul and at times she became very fearful for her young woman. So when she was found, she felt the same relief that her parents felt but also their anger at her not telling them anything. They would go and see her at the foster carers' house that night and take her out for a meal and then the following week plans would be made yet again on how to keep her safe.

John sent a text to say that he was being a very helpful person and she smiled.

A tear trickled down her face as she felt relief that her girl had been found but also remembered her own wedding day. She had tried not to think about it much because she knew that she would just feel sad and the missing girl had kept her busy. While she was in Manchester she had managed not to think too much about it all but now the stresses of the previous weeks returned.

She had been told when she started her training that social work was stressful but it was only after Alan died that it started to affect her and she began to question what she was doing. It wasn't really working with difficult and distressed people that got to her or most of her colleagues, it was the frustrations caused by all the bureaucracy and the lack of resources. There were so many forms to fill in and repetitive reports to write. There were procedures for everything but trying to find a simple phone number could sometimes take so much time that she wondered who had designed these systems. Did they really want robots rather than real people

It wasn't just Steph that felt that way, she didn't know any workers who didn't. She worked with some good social workers but the stress levels were so high that sickness was rife and workers would leave after a few years to take up jobs that meant that they could get home to their kids for tea. She was lucky that she didn't have to worry about whether to jump the speed cameras or be late picking up a tired child from the nursery. Sometimes she longed for her own child but then wondered how her colleagues coped.

"Go home," said Martin. "There is nothing else you can do; if she runs she runs."

Steph had presented her case at the secure unit panel but they still felt that she didn't fill the criteria and that more direct work should be tried first, but Steph wondered if one day her girl would associate with the wrong group and lie dead in a ditch somewhere.

"And then who would get the blame?" Steph had said, feeling so angry and frustrated.

"But you've done all that you can," Martin had said and Steph knew that what he said was true but it just didn't make her feel any better.

"I hope the wedding goes well," said Martin as he and Steph walked to their respective cars.

"Thanks, see you on Monday," she said.

"Had a bad day at work darling?" said John jokingly as Steph kicked off her shoes in the hall. It made her smile.

The rest of the evening flew by and Steph soon found her spirits lifted.

"Time for bed," said John. "You have a busy day tomorrow."

Her parents had gone to bed a hour before but Steph and John had stayed up chatting – well, really reminiscing on the time that they had known each other and all the good and bad things that had happened during that time.

"Do you remember what a pompous prig I used to be?" said John.

Steph smiled when he said this. At the time she had really disliked him, but he had changed so much and become the John that she now knew and she wondered whether, when she was in Manchester, she should have crept into his bed and cuddled up beside him; but she didn't and once again she had lost that opportunity.

Chapter Seventeen

It was a beautiful sunny morning.

"Wakey wakey, princess" said John as he brought Steph a tray laden with goodies.

"If you do this for the bridesmaid, what would you do for the bride?" Steph said sleepily.

"Well," said John with a big grin on his face, "I imagine that I'd give her a good seeing to."

Steph laughed.

"Get out so I can put my dressing gown on," she said sharply.

"Oh modesty," said John in a playful way.

Steph liked this. She felt very happy.

Two hours later they headed off to the church. Steph was surprised that Lucy had decided on such a traditional wedding. She thought that she'd go for something a bit more way out but she did feel a bit like a princess in her long pink velvet dress and John looked very handsome dressed in tails.

"You look a very handsome couple," said Steph's dad as they left. "Have a lovely time."

"Thanks Dad," said Steph and she felt like it was she, not Lucy, that was getting married. She remembered how she felt with Alan but realised that she no longer felt sad she was happy standing next to John.

Lucy had gone for a big traditional wedding with most of her family, old friends and a few people from work. Her team manager Kate was there with her partner. Steph went over to her; John remained talking with one of Lucy's aunties.

"Is that your new bloke then?" said Kate quizzically.

"Oh no, I've known John for a while; he was my lodger for about eighteen months but now lives in Manchester."

"Is he a social worker?"

"No, he's a journalist, but he's very interested in what we do. In fact he's just making a pilot programme around a social work team, which is actually called The Team."

"That's interesting, does he think that it will become a series?"

"I think he hopes so but he's not really sure."

John had finished chatting and came over to Steph and Kate.

"John, this is Kate, Lucy's boss."

"Steph's been telling me about the programme you are making."

"Yes, it's been an exciting project, a bit scary too, though, when your best friend is a social worker." He put his arm around Steph as he said this and Steph noticed that Kate's eyebrows lifted and that she suddenly became very attentive.

"So what's your long-term aim?" said Kate.

"Oh, to live by the sea with the woman I love," said John nonchalantly.

"Sounds nice," said Kate dreamily, "but you'd have to have enough money."

"Yep," said John. "That bestseller would have to keep showing interest and have been made into an epic or long-running series, but then if you don't dream nothing ever comes true, does it?"

"No, I suppose not, but then sometimes in our line of work it is hard to dream when you are hit smack bang in the face by desperation and misery. Half the world just really don't know what we have to deal with and the suffering that people go through on a daily basis."

"What's worse is the bureaucracy though, surely," said Steph, joining in the conversation.

"True," said Kate, "but what can we actually do about that? We are lumbered with an array of forms, and systems that just make you want to scream."

"So it's not just you then, Steph, that gets heated about this subject."

"Oh, come on John. How could you believe that it was just me? I would imagine that most social workers feel this way."

"But so do teachers and nurses."

"But would they stop an operation to fill a form?" said Steph. "We can't visit people in a semi-crisis because with all the bureaucracy there just aren't enough hours in the day."

Kate's partner Frank had joined them during the conversation.

"This is supposed to be a wedding not a funeral," he joked.

Just as he said that the guests were starting to be ushered into the church.

"Do a good job," said John as he kissed Steph on the cheek. "I'll be looking at you floating down the aisle. You do look innocently gorgeous in that dress you know, in fact a bit like candy floss."

Steph smirked at John and tried to tickle him but he had moved too far away.

He smiled back at her, a fabulous smile, which just sent flutters through her heart.

As Steph walked behind Lucy, little did she know that only a few months later that it would be her walking there as the bride. Soon she would have a second chance and this time it would last forever.

The meal after the wedding was a sit-down affair and Steph thought it was a bit disappointing. The speeches were very traditional and the disco afterwards reminded her of an old soppy film. Everyone seemed to enjoy themselves though, so she decided just to go with the flow. But when Lucy's mum started the karaoke Steph found herself in her uncontrollable giggles. The more serious the song the more giggly she got. John stood by with a huge grin on his face.

Chapter Eighteen

"I feel sick," said Steph. "Oh no," and she rushed to the bathroom.

"Oh, my head," she moaned.

"Serves you right," said John, laughing.

Steph's parents had gone to visit a friend and so they had the house to themselves. Steph curled up next to John on the settee and placed the wet flannel which she had brought from the bathroom on her forehead.

"Ouch," she wailed.

"You poor baby," John said, kissing just below the wet flannel.

"It was a good wedding though, we ought to do it," he said.

"What? You and me?" Steph giggled. "Ouch, oh, I feel sick," and the next thing she knew Steph was being violently sick over herself and John.

"Do you still want to marry me?" she said later in the day, when she was feeling rather a lot better.

"Of course I do," said John. "It's not every girl that showers me with puke."

Steph playfully hit him.

"What are you two up to?" said Steph's mum as she came into the living room.

"She didn't notice the smell?" said Steph.

"Good job," said John. "My mum would go mad if you puked up over her carpet."

"You know that you rarely talk about your family."

"Well I suppose we just aren't as close as yours, that's all."

Steph looked at John and felt the way she used to when he lodged with her, that comfortable feeling. She liked it.

That night John lay awake on the settee thinking of Steph upstairs and wondered whether she was fast asleep. He would have liked to creep upstairs and snuggle in beside her but he didn't even try and as dawn began to shine through the slit in the curtains he began to dream.

His dream was muddled with a line of faceless women in front of him. He knew that he was on one side of a river and he knew that Steph was the other side but he couldn't see her. He began to panic and was calling to her but he couldn't find her. He suddenly awoke as Steph's dad tried to creep into the room.

"Sorry to wake you John, but I left both pairs of my specs in here last night and I'm just useless without them, oh there they are," he said, heading towards the small coffee table.

John found that he was wide awake, there was just no way that he could go back into the dream. He remembered talking to Steph about getting married and he shivered with embarrassment.

"She will think me a fool," he thought.

Steph woke suddenly and wondered what day of the week it was. She jumped out of bed thinking that she was going to be late for work and then remembered that she had booked a day off in lieu. She had done so much overtime recently that even with the days that she had had with John in Manchester she was still owed time. Most of the time she, like her colleagues, just accepted that that was the way that you worked. You couldn't just desert a needy child who had nowhere to sleep for the night. But she realised how difficult it was for her colleagues with kids.

She had often wondered why some of the many fit older people couldn't volunteer their services to sit with a kid but then neither she nor anyone else had the energy to set up such a scheme.

She went to get a drink and there was her dear John making his familiar coffee. He would take some proper coffee wherever he went. He said that instant was just not the same. He had had to succumb to coffee bags but had said that they were a good compromise.

"And how's the head?" he said.

"Oh it's fine this morning. What time are you going home?" she said.

"Trying to get rid of me?" he joked.

"Of course not, I'm just thinking of the day, that's all."

She didn't have to think of the day as she didn't have anything particular that she wanted to do and, in fact, now that the weeks of build up to the wedding were over she felt a kind of anti-climax.

The phone rang.

"Is John still with you?" said Martin.

"Yes, why? What's the matter? Martin are you alright, you sound strange."

"Steph, its Mandy," he said hesitating.

"What, she's run again, has she?"

"Yes, but it's worse than that. She ran and was drugged, raped, beaten up and is now in a terrible state in the QE."

Steph was stunned, she just didn't know what to say. "I …" she handed the phone to John. It was just too much. John took the phone and he heard the awful news.

"Are you OK, Martin? Is there anything that I can do?"

"John, the press have got the wind of the story and, you know, our lot are just so hopeless. What do we do?"

"I'll ring Steph's mum at work and come to your office if you like."

"I know that they won't like it but we need you, John."

John rang Steph's mum. He was worried, she had just sat staring into thin air.

"Her dad's coming home too," Mum said, "we'll look after her, you go and help the team."

"I'll have to make a few phone calls first," John said.

Chapter Nineteen

"I'll have to talk to you down here," said Martin. "The management are so fearful of anyone to do with the press being in the building. I must admit, John, that this time I am having my own problems keeping it together. She was such a nice kid who just got in with the wrong crowd and her parents could no longer cope."

"You sound as though she's died," said John.

"She's in a terrible state, really badly beaten up and they don't know how much and what type of drugs she has been given. Her mum wants to tell her story. She rang me and said that the world just had to know but who could she trust to tell. I told her about you ... will you do it, John?"

"Yes," he said, knowing that this might change his life forever.

John was mentally drained when he got back to Steph's house.

"How is she?" he said.

"She hasn't cried yet, I think that she was waiting for you."

"Let's go to the Clent Hills," Steph said to John.

"OK," he said.

They drove silently and reached the base of the hills.

"You were so long," she said.

"I'm writing her story, Steph."

"That's good, the world needs to know ... John, will you do something for me?" she said.

"What's that?" he said, pensively

"Marry me ... I need you John ... I just want to be part of you ... I've always needed and wanted you. You are the only person I feel really safe with ... please marry me," and as she said this she began to cry.

John put his arms around her.

"Of course, I'll marry you," he said. "It's just that, perhaps, I was hoping that it would be a happier proposal, that's all."

49

"Oh, John." Steph said those two words in such a way that just melted John's heart. He knew that whatever happened in life he just always wanted to be near Steph.

John's mobile rang, it was Martin. "Good news," he said "Mandy's going to be OK and she wants to see you to give her part of the story ... how's Steph?"

Steph grabbed the phone off John.

"Martin, I'm fine, I'm so glad that she is OK."

"How did you know?" said Martin.

"Just from John's face, that's all. Oh, and Martin, guess what."

"What?" said Martin, feeling a little more cheery.

"I'm going to marry John."

"Wow," said Martin.

"So it's official then?" said John as she handed back the mobile.

"Why, did you want it to be a secret?"

"No," he just laughed. This was so Steph, the vibrant woman that he loved. He just felt so very happy.

Chapter Twenty

John knew that this was the most important story that he would ever write. The world just had to know the truth. The general public had to take some responsibility; they just couldn't continue to pass the buck. Here was this lovely young woman who might never be able to have any children because of the damage that had been caused to her and, as usual, the tacky press were trying to blame someone else.

Her parents had found her so hard to control. She knew that ultimately she could walk out of their door any time and had contacted Social Services on several occasions to say that she was being abused by them. Once her mum had hit her hard, causing a bruise, and the police had wanted to prosecute but Mandy had later withdrawn the charges and her mum had been so ashamed.

"I will always walk away in the future," she had said.

Mandy was a bright girl who was doing well with her GCSEs but her education was disrupted during her time in care. She had been in a children's home and with three lots of foster parents within a year.

"I thought that I didn't need anybody," she told John.

"I loved my mum and dad but they just didn't understand me."

John had decided to stay with Steph for a week, to see that she was alright but also to write Mandy's story. His boss in Manchester was a bit fed up with him but then he knew how talented John was and he could contact him any time by mobile.

Steph had cried at the top of the Clent Hills and then had run up into the wind. John had experienced every emotion possible that day on those hills and realised how alive he was. They had clung to each other so tightly that at one point Steph wondered whether she would stop breathing.

And now John sat with Mandy and felt so much for her. He suddenly realised that Mandy was one of the faceless people from his dream.

She was a survivor just like Steph and he was honoured to tell her story.

Chapter Twenty-one

"Congratulations, Steph." Everyone around her was so pleased for her.

"You never told us how gorgeous he is," said Sarah.

Steph felt so happy and went around with a smile on her face. She rang John.

"So how's the story going?" she asked him.

"Fine," he said. "By the way…"

"I know what you are going to say … yes, we'll have to tell them tonight, and your lot too."

Steph arrived home to the wonderful smell that she remembered. John was cooking one of his curries.

"They're not home yet," John said.

"They generally work late on a Wednesday," Steph said.

"You're early."

"I got most things done and couldn't face doing any more write-ups … I think I'll go in early tomorrow and try to get some more done. You are going home in the morning, aren't you?"

"Yes, I'll have to … but I really don't want to leave you."

"I know but we've got all the time in the world, my love."

These words sent an excited shiver down John's spine.

"I've nearly finished Mandy's story and the Morning are interested in it."

"Not the Reader then" said Steph quizzingly.

"No, apparently they've done their own… but its not gonna be as good as mine."

"Oh cocky," said Steph smiling. "I saw Mandy today just after you left, she said that she liked you," Steph commented.

"Did you tell her that I was your man?"

"No… I have to keep things separate."

"Yes, I suppose, but I'm just so excited about you and me."

Steph's parents arrived home together; they had met at Wickes to get some tiles for the bathroom. Steph's dad had promised to replace the existing ones several years ago when they moved to the house and at last he was getting on with the job.

"Nice smell," said Dad, "any for us?"

"Of course," said John. "Well, it's about time that I did my share … It's ready whenever you are."

They sat down and Mum talked about her day and asked how Mandy was and how John's article was getting on. John had also made a pudding, which they all thought was scrummy.

"It's a pity that you're not here more regularly," said Mum.

"Well, he might be," said Steph. "Oh, John, are you going to tell them or me?"

"What she's saying is that we are getting married … right, I've said it."

Steph's parents leapt out of their seats and hugged John and Steph respectively. They were over the moon. And then John appeared with a bottle of champagne.

"When?" said Mum, all excited.

"Oh, I don't know. We haven't even jumped into bed with each other yet," said Steph.

"Oh, she's so sordid … what am I gonna do with her?" said John smiling.

"Give me a good seeing to," Steph whispered as she held him close.

"That would be nice," he whispered back.

"So where's your engagement ring then?" said Mum.

"Oh Mum, we've got better things to spend money on than that," said Steph.

"Have we?" said John, sheepishly pulling a little box from the pocket of his sweatshirt.

"It's an opal," said Steph.

"Well, you are a Libran after all and have often commented that you hated diamonds… shall I change it?"

"Of course not… I love it."

Steph proudly wore her opal and wondered what future adventures lay ahead with her John.

"So when are you telling your parents?"

"Oh, I was hoping that Steph could come with me to see them at the weekend."

"Cor blimey, after all of this time I am going to meet your parents."

"Yes, but don't blame me for who they are."

This sounded ominous and Steph wondered what John meant by this.

She wouldn't have to wait for long as it was now Wednesday and they were to go to stay with them on the Friday and Saturday night. Steph would go up to Manchester and then John was going to drive them to their house.

After tea the four of them sat down for a game of mah-jong. Steph had introduced her parents to the game after John had taught her. They often used to ask David and Ian around for a game. David used to love shouting out when he got a pung. "Oh, doesn't it sound great?" he would squeal.

Steph missed those days. She wondered about the other men that had been in her life and she suddenly thought of Mark who she had only been out with a few weeks ago. She had had a nice time and had promised him another date. She wondered what he would think of her now. She made her mind up to have a chat with him the next day.

That night, after her mum and dad went to bed, Steph sat with John on the settee.

"I love you," said John, "and I am so glad that you are going to marry me. I just have one problem."

"What's that?"

"I want to snuggle up with you and, well, I just can't do it here under your parents' roof."

"Why not?" Steph said.

"I dunno."

As she said this Dad appeared in the doorway.

"Mum and I have just had a chat," he said, "and, well, we think its rather silly John sleeping here on the settee and in some ways rather a nuisance and so we think that as you have plenty of room that he should join you, Steph. And don't be too late you two, Steph has work in the morning and you've got to go and catch up on yours John. Night, see you in the morning."

"Well, what do you feel now?" Steph said with a sexy smile all over her face.

"I think that unless you object that I'd like to give you a good seeing to."

Steph whispered that she really had no objection at all.

Chapter Twenty-two

It was so nice lying in John's arms that she really didn't want to get up.

"Oh, I wish I could just stay here all day," she moaned.

"Me, too," said John. "But we won't solve the world's problems lying in each other's arms."

"But we could lie here and send out love waves to the world and solve them that way. We could be a love energy factory, developing gallons of love potions and sending them down the rivers into the drinking water. We could then send them through the television and internet airwaves."

"Yes, it would be so nice if we could do that, just like a witch's spell," John remarked.

They got dressed and went downstairs together.

"Mum's had to go, she had an early meeting," Dad said, as he buttered his toast.

"Did you sleep well?"

"Yes," they both said together.

"Well I'm off in a mo too. When do we see you again John?"

"I'm not sure, I've got quite a lot of things that I have neglected in Manchester and so I'm hoping that Steph can come up there instead. We are going to meet my parents at the weekend anyhow."

Steph drove to work feeling very happy. She had a busy day ahead of her but she knew that she could cope. She had survived the bad days and so ones like today were just nothing to compare. She had two child protection conferences. The first was an initial conference concerning two young children who were suffering neglect. It was quite a tricky case as the mother had a learning disability and, although she was having quite a lot of professional input she just didn't seem to have a clue without prompting on what her children needed.

Casey was three and Louise was only eight months old. Their dad also had a learning disability and a temper. If he didn't get his own way he would get into a tantrum. The case was only just coming to Steph's team. She would pick it up straight from the conference.

The second was a mother with a mental health problem. She had two young children, two girls, aged three and one year old. She was only twenty-three years old and it was a sad case as her mental illness was attributed to the birth of her children. She had been sectioned under the Mental Health Act and was at the local hospital on a psychiatric ward. Her children were living with her older sister and her husband as their father was in prison and wasn't due out for another year.

The reason the children were on the register was because she had neglected them for several days when she became ill and her sister was on holiday. A neighbour had contacted the NSPCC. It was a sad case as apparently, when she was well, she was a really good mum but this was her second episode in hospital and, whereas last time she was there for about a month, this time she had already been there for three months and didn't seem to be getting any better. Both of the children were beginning to regard her sister as their mum and were reserved when they were taken to see her.

The sister was doing well with the children but she had four young children of her own and so it was hard work, especially as she also worked part time as a secretary.

"I don't know how they manage it," Steph said later that night when she talked to John on the phone.

The conference went OK. The children's names remained on the register as there was still felt to be a risk to the children if their mum was discharged and was unable to care for them. Steph wondered what the children made of it all. She wondered what they would remember when they grew up if their mum got well.

"What if she never gets better?" Steph had said to Martin after the conference.

"You can't think like that Steph."

"But Martin, it could be true and it's such a lot of pressure on her sister and her husband."

"They want to do it Steph, and we can just help them in any way that we can. You would do the same if it was someone in your family, wouldn't you?"

She knew that she would, but still found it sad. She had to keep a clear head, keep reasonably detached the way that she had been taught at uni but she was still human and at times keeping detached was difficult.

She remembered some of the lecturers and how her fellow students would criticise them, saying that as they hadn't practised for donkeys' years how did they know what it was like out there in the field. She had thought it a strange word and had had visions of green fields with cattle; amongst them were a few bulls.

Some of what she had learnt at uni was useful but there was so much that she just had to learn by experience and at times she was embarrassed, disappointed, angry but sometimes she would smile as she had truly helped someone change behaviour and be much happier for it.

She thought of the family who always rowed with each other and sometimes these rows would become physical. Social Services had got involved when Tom, the seven-year-old son of Tina and Geoff, got injured when he came to protect his mum during one of these rows. Nine months later Steph started preparing a report for a child protection conference and she was pleased because the adults in the extended family not only had begun to realise the impact of their lifestyle on Tom but were also trying actively to do something about it. Yes, she was pleased that the work that she had been doing with them was actually having some impact. There were just so many times when nothing seemed to change or any change was only for a short time and then people would fall back into their own ways.

That afternoon she had to attend a FAP, a funding application panel. She had a young asylum seeker who was currently living with private foster carers outside Birmingham and she had to seek further funding. He was seventeen years old and had arrived in the UK on the back of a lorry illegally when he was fourteen years old. He had gone into hiding but had eventually been picked up by the police in Birmingham.

He was a nice young man who had become fluent in both spoken and written English and was currently in college. Steph had read his story and wondered how immigration found out whether it was true or not. After nearly three years his case hadn't even been heard yet, which he found so frustrating.

"Steph, you need to update his pathway plan and his core assessment," the chair of the panel said. "OK," Steph replied, thinking of the mounds of paperwork she had waiting for her.

"He needs to move, Steph, There is no reason why he still needs to be with foster parents. Just because they won't have him on a supported lodgings basis isn't a good enough reason for him to be there. We'll see you back at FAP in three months' time and expect some progress."

Steph left the panel relieved that the funding was continued but irritated by the "school marm" approach that the panel members had presented. She sympathised with them. She knew that it was about keeping costs down and the paperwork helped with the star ratings but more paperwork meant less contact than she had and currently all of her cases needed that extra nurturing that only she could give.

She walked back to the office and stopped at the nice sandwich shop to get a cheese and beetroot sandwich. It was rather late but she was hungry and probably wouldn't get any tea as she had a late visit to one of her foster children.

She liked doing social work but sometimes it was just so over-demanding. She thought about the woman who so carefully prepared her sandwich. She wondered what time she would get home and what she would then have to do. She always produced the most delicious sandwiches, carefully wrapped in greaseproof paper. Yes, sometimes she wished that she could do that but then thought that she just couldn't do them so well.

What did this woman think about as she made those gorgeous preparations? She never seemed bored, she was always so conscientious.

"Hello, how are you, Steph?" said a voice.

Steph looked around and saw one of the clerks from the legal department."

"I don't seem to have had any cases from you for ages."

"No," said Steph pensively.

"How are you anyhow? I don't think I've seen you since..." and he hesitated, meaning since the death of Alan and Paul.

"I'm fine, actually very happy. It was tough after Alan and Paul died but it's amazing what life brings. In fact, I very recently got engaged."

"Oh that's nice, who to?"

"Did you want pepper?" said the sandwich maker.

"Yes please," said Steph. "Someone I have known for some time; he used to be my lodger and then he moved to Manchester. We were always good friends and it's just kind of grown from there."

"Oh I'm so pleased," he said. "I often wondered how you were doing, but life is so hectic and I hadn't seen you and didn't really want to ask your colleagues."

"And how are things for you?" said Steph. "Last time I spoke to you, your wife wasn't very well, how is she?"

"She died six weeks ago."

"Oh I'm so sorry."

"She had been ill for two years, as you know."

"And how are the children?" said Steph sympathetically.

"They aren't taking it very well. Tom, who is ten, gets upset a lot at school and Jenny, who is sixteen, spends most of her time away from home. And I get so lonely, Steph." Clive started to cry as he said this.

The other sandwich maker quickly finished his sandwich and asked for the money.

"Look, Clive, let's sit in the square for a few minutes and eat our sandwiches. I have done a lot for Social Services today and haven't had a lunch break. I don't want you going back like this."

"OK," said Clive. "But I better just ring the office as I said that I'd only be a couple of minutes."

Steph was amazed how Clive was able to put on a calm, competent voice when inside he was so obviously crumbling.

"Have you had some time off with the children?" Steph said.

"I had a couple of weeks after Clare died but when I returned there was just so much I had to catch up on."

They sat in the little park that had a stream running through it. Steph could hear the soothing sound of it running over pebbles. They were the only people there and for a moment it felt like they were the only people in the world and then the familiar sound of a text arriving was heard from her phone, she ignored it and Clive didn't seem to hear it.

Steph listened to Clive talking about life without Clare and what it was like being both mum and dad to the children. Although Clare had been physically ill for sometime she had still very much been part of all of their lives and now Clive just felt this emptiness and Steph knew exactly what he felt.

She sympathised with his feelings when he said that people said that at least he had the children. But that just wasn't the same as having Clare.

Steph walked back to the office, Clive seemed calmer as he left. She looked at the text, which was from John. He was excited because his programme was to be on the TV a month later. She remembered how fabulous she felt in his arms and hoped that one day Clive would be able to feel that way again.

Chapter Twenty-three

Steph thought of Clive as she sat on the train to Manchester. What would his weekend be like? She then thought about her own weekend. She was about to meet John's parents and he had talked in a way as if there was something strange about them. She knew that they lived in a mobile home but she didn't know much else about them.

She came into Manchester Piccadilly, which was becoming a familiar place to her, and saw John standing on the platform. It had taken some time for them to be honest about how they felt about each other but now a sense of calm came over her.

"How was the journey?" John said as he hoisted Steph's bag over his shoulder. "I've got a surprise for you," he said.

"What?" she said.

"Just wait and see," he said.

They walked to the car park and Steph looked for John's car but instead he flashed his car key at a little car up in the corner.

"That's yours?" she said with a big grin on her face.

"Yes, I thought it was easier for me to get around Manchester." John had bought a Smart car.

"Its very comfy," said Steph as they headed off to John's house, "and it's got an open top."

"Yes," John grinned and opened the top with the electric button.

Steph's hair blew in the breeze. It was a warm June evening.

"So when are we going to see your mum and dad?"

"In the morning. I thought that we could have a nice quiet evening on our own. Do you want to eat in or out?"

"I don't mind, you choose."

"Let's eat in then."

"That would be nice and we could get an early night," Steph said with a glint in her eye.

"Sounds like heaven," John murmured.

The next morning Steph woke and found the sunshine streaming in through the curtains. John was still fast asleep and so she quietly pulled one of the curtains open so that she could peep into the back garden. The garden was only big enough for a couple of deckchairs and a whirlygig washing line. Sitting on the washing line was a robin. She had seen him in the garden before.

John murmured and Steph looked at him and smiled. How sweet he looked, she thought. He had pushed most of the duvet off so she could see his strong firm chest. She remembered how he had often stood in a pair of shorts at her house and she had admired that body. Her own seemed so inadequate in comparison and recently she had put a little too much weight on.

She had moaned to Lucy that she only lost weight when she was miserable. After Alan died she had lost quite a bit of weight and everyone was constantly trying to feed her up.

"I love you whatever size you are," John had said.

The robin hopped around the garden but then a cat came into the garden and it quickly flew away.

Steph decided that she would rather be a robin than a cat.

"Hello you," said John sleepily.

Steph leant over and kissed him.

"So we meet at last," said John's mum giving Steph a huge hug.

"We've heard so much about you."

"Well, Mum, Steph and I are getting married."

"Oh, are you sure?" said his Mum in a worried way. "You know what it did to me and your father, we are so much better now we are divorced."

"But you still live together, Mum."

"Of course we do, you silly."

Steph was rather confused but she thought that it wasn't the time for an explanation.

"I hope you like spinach," said John's dad as he walked in carrying an armful."

Steph wasn't very keen but she thought she'd just put up with it on this occasion.

"They are getting married," said John's mum.

"Splendid," said John's dad with a hearty grin. "P'raps you and I should get married again, old girl," he said wrapping his arms around John's mum.

They talked a lot about the garden and after their vegetarian lunch were taken off for a walk.

"Steph, you can borrow my pair of spare wellies," said John's mum.

"Thanks," she said and they all headed down a muddy path.

An hour later they returned to the mobile home feeling tired and thirsty.

"Nettle tea anyone?"

"Oh, Mum, you don't have to go to extremes"

John's mum chuckled. "Well, everyone expects us to have such things. I can't help it if I like my Nescafe and your dad his Typhoo."

"Steph doesn't drink tea or coffee."

"We've got some orange barley, will that do?"

"That would be lovely," said Steph feeling a little tired.

"Why don't you have a little nap before tea," said Mum.

Steph lay on the double bed and snuggled under the blanket. John had decided to stay with his mum and chat. Steph dozed off and found herself dreaming but she didn't really understand what the dream was about.

When she awoke she lay just looking at the strange, cramped room. She wondered why John's parents had given up a large Victorian house in a nice part of Manchester to come and live in Wales in a mobile home. They were several miles from a local shop.

It was nice snuggling under the blanket and she found it difficult to move but eventually dragged herself up as she was dying for the toilet.

"Did you have a nice snooze?" John's mum said.

"Yes, thanks, the trouble was that I just didn't want to move."

"It's the air here, it's so nice and clear. John and his dad have popped into town to get some chicken wire. John said that he would help repair the coop as we had two escapees recently. I expect you wonder why we gave up a large house in Manchester to come and live here?" She didn't wait for a reply. "We both had good responsible jobs and were looking towards having a good pension and retirement but one day we woke up and both said practically at the same time that we wanted to do something else. We didn't have any kids at home any more and that night we found this piece of land on the internet. It was as if it was meant to be."

"And has it worked out the way that you expected?" said Steph enquiringly.

"Mostly, yes."

"But why did you get divorced but carry on living together?"

"We wanted to know that we were free, if we needed to be."

Steph didn't understand this.

John and his Dad arrived back.

"You should have a go in the Smartie," John's dad said "it's really good fun."

Steph looked across at Katie whose parents loved her so much but found her so hard to care for. She thought it was just not fair. Katie had been born with a rare disability that left her blind and severely mentally handicapped. Her parents Rod and Louise had tried for years to have a child and when Louise became pregnant they were so happy.

After Katie was born there were concerns that she wasn't feeding properly and the GP and health visitor began to think that Louise and Rod were neglecting her. A case conference was called and Katie was put on the Child Protection register, that was six years ago and for a while the concentration was on the parents as carers but then a new social worker took over the case and felt that there just hadn't been enough investigations into Katie's medical condition.

Now Steph sat with Rod and Louise reviewing what support they needed for Katie. As they talked Katie tried to join in the conversation but all that Steph could make out were unfamiliar noises. Steph had managed to find a good carer for Katie who would look after her for a weekend every month to give Louise and Rod a break.

When she had first met the family Louise had said how distressing the early days had been; she said that it was hard enough dealing with Katie's disability but to also be accused of impeding her development was just so cruel. Steph felt so sad for them and felt that she had the guilt of Social Services on her shoulders.

"But you can't feel like that," John had said. "Do you think that journalists carry the burden of all their mistakes on their shoulders?"

"But that's not the point," Steph had said.

"You can only do your best with the resources that you have."

"But workers should think more, they should think what it would feel like to them if they were Louise and Rod, and the medics just didn't do their job."

Steph thought of this conversation and of the strange weekend that she had had with John's parents. John had seemed to be embarrassed by their lifestyle but she had thought that they seemed to be nice people and loved their son and had made her very welcome.

She had really enjoyed playing cards with them in the evening and the tea had been delicious. She definitely felt that veg taken straight from the garden was far superior.

Chapter Twenty-four

"I miss you so much" said John. "Can't someone else do the contact visits?"

"I have to observe the family for the court reports. I only have one more visit."

"But why does it have to be done on a Saturday?"

"Because the parents work and with so many children to see, well, that was the easiest way to manage it."

"I wish I could come down but I'm just so busy."

"John, I miss you too and love you; this will soon be over."

"I just hoped you'd be here with me on Monday. What if it's a flop, what if…"

"Don't think like that John…"

Steph felt pulled; she had so much work to do with the Green family. They had seven children and there were concerns about the parenting of all of them and the domestic violence within which they operated as a family.

She wanted to be with John but had to go to court on Tuesday and so wouldn't be able to get back in time. She knew how important the drama was to him. He had been involved with it for so long and it was like his baby but it was a drama and she was working with the real people. He could write in changes to his characters lives but she would have to convince the court that so many things had been tried and even though she felt sorry for the parents, they had shown that they were just unwilling to change and that the children needed a better deal in life.

Steph wasn't the kind of social worker who believed in taking children into care but there had been so much long-term abuse on the Green children and when Kylie was found drunk at the age of six from drinking her parents whisky it was just the last straw.

"We can't ignore it," Martin had said to Steph. "And it's not the first time."

"I know," Steph replied.

The police, in the end, had to do a PPO and, out of hours, had been driven to distraction by having to place seven children. Mr Green had gone to the press but fortunately the local editor had seen the reality of the situation.

And now the Greens were undergoing therapy and wanted the children back and so Steph had to undertake these long, detailed assessments. She had mixed feelings but on balance felt that the Greens were just not ready.

"Why don't you come and watch it here with me?" Steph said.

"OK, but it would have been nicer for us to be alone. I really like your mum and dad but..."

Steph felt pressured and pulled; she wanted to be with John but wanted to do a good job too.

"I think you're mad," said Lucy. "John is such a fab guy, you should just marry him and go and live in Manchester. He's beginning to make a lot more money so you could give up work and stay at home and have babies. You are not getting any younger you know."

Steph cringed at Lucy's patronising tone. It was true she was well into her thirties and if she wanted kids would soon have to get on with it but if she and John had a child like Katie would they cope, she thought.

Sometimes doing social work gave Steph depressing thoughts but she could usually work through them very quickly. The public just didn't know how pressured and emotionally charged the work was.

A few weeks after Steph told Mark about her and John, Mark had gone off long-term sick and was apparently having a complete nervous breakdown. She never wanted to get like that; she would leave before that happened – but would she, that kind of thing just crept on you.

"But surely there just couldn't be anything worse than losing Alan and Paul," she thought but she realised that there was; losing John would be worse.

"When the Green case is over I want some time in lieu," Steph said.

"You'll need about a week for all that extra time you've taken Steph; I told you to take some time," Martin said.

"But you know how busy I've been."

"Well, we are going to book it now and I think that you should go and book a holiday with John, out of the country."

"Shall I find something then?" Steph said to John, holding the mobile in one hand and her cheese and beetroot sandwich in the other.

"Yes," said John.

They agreed the date and Steph promised to take a lunch break one day and go and book something. They knew that where they went didn't matter.

The kids were still on school holidays and so there might not be many deals. They just wanted to be together.

Steph went into the travel agents and asked for last-minute deals. There was one that looked OK in the Costa Brava. She rang John but got the answer phone and so she decided just to book it anyhow.

"Can you go on a joint visit to the Francis family please?" said Martin.

"Can't anyone else do it?" Steph said. "You know I've got so much to do."

"No, it's a dangerous situation and the police are going to be there as well; it'll probably be a PPO."

"Martin, this is just ridiculous. You know I wouldn't normally say anything but something's got to be done about the staffing. What will you do when I'm on holiday? Martin, don't look at me in that way."

Martin had his pathetic pleading look on but the thing was that Steph knew that part of the reason why she was going was that Sarah was hopeless in these situations. She was very good at therapeutic work but when it was a crisis she was hopeless and was unable to work effectively with the police.

Most of the work these days was liaising with different professionals and Steph had a talent which most of her colleagues were envious of. Other professionals would just bend over backwards to help.

"I'm just honest and nice with them that's all," she would tell them, but surely there was more than that.

Chapter Twenty-five

"Thank God it's you coming," said DI Thompson.

"Why are you here and not uniform police?" Steph queried down the mobile.

"It's rather sensitive stuff."

Sarah had said that she would drive and Steph could talk to the police.

"Can you meet me in the Grove so I can speak to you beforehand?" said DI Thompson.

"OK."

Steph knew that it was sod's law. Her team were covering duty for the Assessment team because they were on an away day. They skirted past the Newcross Hotel and saw loads of photographers waiting outside.

"What the heck is going on?" said Sarah.

"Beats me," said Steph, who suddenly felt very alert. She liked a different challenge and this certainly seemed to be the case.

They parked in the Grove and Steph spotted DI Thompson. She had worked on a case with him over a year ago and was trying to remember his first name.

"Hi Steph. This is an unusual one because it involves a celebrity who is visiting from the states so it is even more complicated. It is Ruby Stringer visiting the UK for the opening night of her latest film, which is in a couple of days' time. She has brought her daughter with her and apparently this morning, when her breakfast was delivered to her room, the hotel member of staff witnessed her severely beating the child."

"How old is she?"

"Three."

"And the injuries?"

"We haven't got in yet as Ms Stringer wouldn't let us into the room and so we are currently applying for a warrant to get into the room. The other problem is that we think that someone from the hotel has tipped the media off and so the hotel is chock-a-block with press."

"And the child, has anyone been able to hear her crying?"

"No, and that's the worry. We have police on the roof and don't think that the window to the room is dangerous so she's not likely to jump."

"Mike, why don't you just break down the door?" said Steph, suddenly remembering DI Thompson's first name.

"I would, but it's not that easy."

Steph suddenly felt worried for the child, whose name was Carly. It sounded as though her mother had really flipped her lid.

"It's the American bit as well, Steph, we just don't know what to do in that situation."

"Mike we have to see the kid, that's the most important bit. I'm going to ring Martin and then we need to go in."

Steph rang the office but couldn't get through.

"Damn," she said.

She then remembered that for some reason John had Martin's mobile number. She rang John.

"Look, I'm in a crisis; its OK, it's not me but have you still got Martin's mobile number?"

John gave her the number and she rang his mobile but it was switched off.

"This is bloody stupid," she said.

"Come with us," said Mike.

They left Sarah's car in the Grove and went in the police detective car.

Getting out of the car was a shock with cameras flashing everywhere.

Mike ushered the two social workers through the cordons of press. Steph felt extremely vulnerable as if she was about to be attacked by vultures.

Hidden behind a row of police Steph rang the office again; she still couldn't get through and Martin's phone was switched off.

"Do you know any other numbers, Steph?"

"The headquarters number," she replied.

"You better ring it then," Mike said.

Steph rang the number and spoke to the receptionist. She asked who of the managers was in the building and said that it was an emergency and that she couldn't get either her manager or office. The secretary grumpily agreed to put her through to the deputy director who seemed preoccupied.

"Perhaps you should wait until your manager is available," he said and appeared not really listening to what she was saying.

"She might be dead for all we know," she replied. "The police haven't heard any noises and they have set up a listening device."

"You'd better go in then," he said. "Which hotel is it? I had better get over there if it is full of press," his voice suddenly sounded panicky.

Steph decided to quickly ring John.

"Ask the police if Tom Stevens is amongst the press. If he is I'll speak to him, he'll keep them under control."

Steph relayed the message to Mike and explained quickly who John was.

"Are you ready then Steph? We have got the warrant."

Steph suddenly felt very panicky and had really forgotten that Sarah was with her. She asked Sarah if she was ready. Sarah looked as nervous as she felt.

"Yes," said Steph quietly and remembered the day when she had to talk the woman from jumping out of the window. There was just no time to delay.

The door was broken down with the hotel manager standing by. Steph, Sarah and Mike went in, there wasn't a sound and then they heard some murmuring. It sounded a little like wailing and was coming from the bathroom.

Steph went ahead opened the door and saw a mass of body. She was unable to distinguish mother from child.

"Ruby, I'm Steph," said Steph gently, "is Carly OK?"

"No," was the reply. Ruby was rocking gently.

Sarah stood by. Mike was about to come forward but Steph signalled for him to stay away. Steph crouched down next to Ruby.

"She's sleeping too much," Ruby said.

Steph saw that Ruby was covered in blood.

"I need to give her a plaster because she's bleeding. Pass her to me," said Steph forcefully.

Amazingly Ruby started to move but then stopped.

"She wouldn't do what I told her," she said. Steph ignored what Ruby was saying. "Tell all the people to go away."

"I'll tell everyone to go except the doctor; she has to help Carly to wake up."

Ruby didn't protest. "I'm too sleepy to argue," she said.

"Have you taken some medicine?" said Steph. Spying a bottle of pills nearby.

Ruby started to slump.

"Mike, we need two doctors now," Steph ordered.

"You will look after Carly for me won't you" said Ruby in a slurred tone, "and her father must not go near her."

"Yes," said Steph and held out her arms to take Carly.

Chapter Twenty-six

When Steph got home John was there. He had driven straight from Manchester to be with her. She cuddled up to him on the settee and told him all about it.

She had expected the worst but found that although badly injured Carly was still breathing. Her body was very limp when she passed her to the paramedic and doctor. She wasn't sure how they had got her out of the hotel. Steph had been taken out under a blanket through the back door but was still aware of flashes from cameras.

She felt safe in John's arms. She was so lucky as he was always there for her.

Mum brought her a large glass of sherry and as she sipped it she felt drowsy.

She didn't eat much that night and was glad when it was time to snuggle up next to John. She fell into a deep slumber and found herself reliving the events in the hotel. Ruby was telling her not, to let Carly's dad near her.

The dream became a nightmare and she suddenly sat up.

"I need to find out if she is alright or not," Steph cried.

"Who?" said John.

"Ruby, it's so important, she has a story to tell."

John thought that Steph was still dreaming but she insisted so he said that he would ring one of his ex-colleagues and find out who was at the hospital.

After some phone calls John was able to tell Steph that both Carly and Ruby were off the critical list.

Steph went into work feeling rather drained from the previous day's events.

"Have you seen the papers?" said Martin.

"No," said Steph.

Martin showed her a copy of the Guardian. The front page showed an idyllic picture of Ruby and Carly and next to it was a picture of the deputy director. The headline read, "And all in a day's work".

The deputy director was interviewed and talked about it all being part of social work; there was no mention of the two social workers who had attended the scene. There was also a personal profile of the deputy director.

John rang. "What a bloody cheek," he said. "He's using the press to sing his own praises but by what you said he wasn't very supportive to you."

"John, it really doesn't matter."

"But it does," he said angrily.

"You are getting too personal, just leave it. I've got to go, bye, love you."

But he wouldn't let it go.

"It just makes the public think that anyone can do it. But they can't, there are not many people who could take the pressures that you have taken Steph and just get no reward for it."

"You are my reward John," said Steph, and said that she had to go.

"The deputy director wants to meet with you and me at 2pm," said Martin. "I think that I'm going to get a ticking off."

Steph found it hard to concentrate for the rest of the morning and had lots of people to contact but everyone seemed to want to talk for a long time. Her phone beeped and there was a text from John.

"Come and live with me in Manchester," it read. "Marry me now."

Steph ignored it and then a few minutes later another one came that said, "Please."

Steph replied that she had things to finish here first.

She wondered whether she had doubts about her and John. Was he trying to be too controlling? Was he trying to protect her but was it really suffocating her? She really wasn't sure.

"Are you ready?" said Martin.

"In a mo," said Steph.

They drove in Martin's car and parked in the headquarters car park. They were lucky to get a space, it was a rare occurrence.

As Martin thought, the deputy director started to have a go at him about not being available. Steph listened to this barrage of complaints and then intervened.

"I haven't got the time to listen to this," she said. "This guy," referring to Martin, "works his socks off and is the best manager I have ever had. I expect that he was told to switch his mobile off as he was at a briefing. There was another manager at the office but I couldn't get through, so don't go complaining about him."

This stopped the deputy director in his tracks and the conversation went on to analyse what had happened. It appeared that he had been telephoned by an anonymous person who was trying to remove Social Services' involvement in the case. "But we are talking about child protection here," said Martin. "We have a child who has been seriously injured by her mother and we need to investigate and protect her."

"We are being told that she is American so there is nothing we can do."

"What about Victoria Climbie then?" said Steph.

Martin and Steph drove back to the office and both felt so aggrieved, but they knew that the law was on their side. The act was carried out on UK land and as such meant that Carly should be protected like any other child.

"Martin, Ms Stringer refuses to see anyone except Steph," said the manager of the Assessment team. "Can you release her for this one?"

"She has to go to court tomorrow but could do a brief visit today."

"Thanks."

Steph couldn't believe it. "She's just playing the prima donna, she is an actress after all."

"But we need the assessment done; I'll get Jane to back your work up."

"But she's only a student, Martin."

"I know Steph, please go with me on this one."

Steph knew what pressure Martin was under; she often wondered how he coped and so submitted. She quickly jotted down people that she needed to contact and sat with Jane filling her in.

"Ring me if you get stuck, I'll only have the phone switched off while I'm at the hospital."

"Its alright, Steph we'll help her," said Sarah.

Suddenly the team seemed to be working together instead of in their separate worlds. It had taken the plight of a celebrity and her daughter to reach this level of cooperation.

Chapter Twenty-seven

Steph arrived at the hospital and found a large number of the press camping outside. She walked past them knowing that they didn't know who she was and who she was visiting.

Ruby Stringer lay in bed and appeared to be dozing. She recognised Steph.

"I'm glad you could come," she said.

"You didn't give me much option," Steph replied.

"Sorry, but I had to talk to you and no one else."

"Why?" said Steph, not really interested in what Ruby had to say.

"I consulted my psychic who said that it had to be you. She said that we had a link, a mission, that I just had to keep in touch with you and you were the only one who could help me and Carly. I really love her, you know, and I just don't know what happened to me and I am so frightened. She is the most important thing in the world to me."

"She is not a thing," said Steph angrily. "She is a human being and she has rights."

"I'm sorry," said Ruby, who suddenly seemed fearful.

Steph felt angry not with either Ruby or Carly but with the weakness of her bosses, their inability to say no. She shouldn't be doing this, she was only filling in for the Assessment team and now it was their job.

"Carly will stay in the hospital until we have carried out an assessment and the police have decided whether to prosecute you or not."

"I know," said Ruby, remorsefully. "I am guilty and I need treatment, but her father is worse than me, he mustn't get custody of her."

"Is his name on her birth certificate?"

"Yes, but we aren't married, he is a monster."

Steph suddenly realised that Ruby was not acting, she was telling what she saw as the truth. Steph knew nothing of US child law but felt that as Carly was in the UK she should be protected by British law and that a full investigation should take place. She told Ruby that she would be back to see her later in the day and advised her to contact a solicitor.

Steph was surprised that Ruby and Carly were in the UK on their own. She always had the view that famous actresses had an entourage with them, but this didn't seem to be the case.

Ruby had told her that both of her parents were dead and that she had been brought up by an aunt. She had run away from home at a young age and had fended for herself.

"I can't suss her out, John," said Steph as she ate a custard tart. She hadn't had one for ages but just couldn't resist today.

"You don't think that she is a monster then?" John replied.

"No, I think it was a single incident of rage, but the paediatricians will be examining Carly closely and taking x-rays. Her father is due in the UK later tonight."

Later, Steph discussed with Martin what Ruby had said about Carly's father.

"She could be just vindictive," he commented.

"True," said Steph pensively, "but she could also be right."

"How is Carly?" said Martin.

"Badly bruised, but nothing is broken."

As they were talking the phone rang; it was Mike, the DI. He said that there was a new development. Ruby claimed that the man she said was Carly's father wasn't her real father.

"So what are we talking about then?" said Martin to Mike.

"I see."

Steph sat trying to follow the conversation. A strategy meeting was set up for later that afternoon as Carly's father was to arrive in the UK. The deputy director was informed about the meeting and decided to come and chair it himself.

Steph sat listening to the contributors not knowing how to feel. She believed in people being given a second chance but was this the first time that Ruby had become so violent? If she had been violent before would she tell Steph?

For now Carly was safe, but there were so many unanswered questions. What this case showed was that protecting children was so crucial and no one, not even a Hollywood film star, was above the law, or was she?

Steph found it hard to sleep. So much was buzzing around in her head.

What did Ruby mean about them having a mission? All that she tried to do was to be a good social worker and to keep children with their parents as much as possible.

It was agreed at the strategy meeting to apply for an interim care order as an EPO wouldn't allow enough time for Carly to get well and carry out a core assessment.

Steph lay there wondering how you could do a core assessment of a child who lived in the USA. She would have to ask Ruby about other relatives and if Ruby's father wouldn't agree to a paternity test, well this would just complicate things further. It was agreed that initially Martin and Steph would work closely together on the case because of the complexity and possible press intrusion.

The hall clock struck 5am. Steph had tossed and turned for most of the night and now just felt exhausted. She thought of John, who was probably fast asleep in bed, and wished that he was there. He had gone back because he had so much to do.

"Perhaps I should give it all up and just be his wife," she thought. But she quickly dismissed this as she knew that this is what she wanted to do and for some reason she had to be the one who helped Carly and perhaps Ruby too.

The next thing she knew was that she heard the alarm. It was seven thirty and she had to get up to see what adventures she was faced with today. She didn't see it as a burden; no, it was an adventure and she was privileged to help change lives. Could she change Ruby's?

Chapter Twenty-eight

It had been a tough couple of weeks with an unbearable caseload. Steph hadn't seen much of John but she knew how important his drama was and she wanted to be there with him to watch it. She had negotiated with Martin to have a few days of time in lieu. Carly was staying with foster carers and it had been proven that Carly's father wasn't the man that claimed to be her father. Steph felt happy about going as Ruby was working very cooperatively with her.

The now so familiar journey to Manchester didn't seem too long. John couldn't meet Steph as he had a meeting about a new project. Steph wasn't sure what it was about but knew that it was very different to the drama.

She caught the bus and walked the short distance to John's house. She always had a key and so she let herself in. After taking her bag upstairs she went into the kitchen to get herself a drink and was faced with an array of flowers and good luck cards. She suddenly realised that John had a whole life that she had no part of and felt a strong pang of jealousy. "What if he had a secret woman and led a double life?" she thought and as she thought this the phone rang. She answered it and heard the familiar tones, the voice that she had come to love so much.

"Yes, the journey was fine; you've got a stack of flowers here."

John was going to be another couple of hours and so he said that they could eat out if Steph liked and still be back for 9pm. The drama was in two parts today and tomorrow and apparently there was a party after the second part either to celebrate or commiserate.

Steph decided to curl up and have a snooze. She set the alarm by the bed so that she wouldn't sleep too long. She threw a travel blanket over herself which they kept in the bedroom, shut her eyes and drifted off. She went into a very muddled dream. Ruby was there and told her that she was going out with John and that she wanted Steph to come along as her nanny. She found herself accepting the situation but feeling sad that John didn't want her any more. She awoke and found John sitting looking at her.

"How long have you been there?" she said.

"Only a few minutes, you looked so peaceful."

"I was having the most awful dream. You were going out with Ruby rather than me."

"Oh dear," said John, "and how did you feel?"

"Very sad."

John laughed and put his arms around Steph; she often had the most vivid dreams. He rarely remembered his own.

"I managed to get away earlier than I thought. I was going to have a bath, do you want to join me?"

Of course, the phone rang while they were in the bath.

John put the answer phone on while the kettle boiled. Steph was drying her hair. There was a call from a woman saying that she was looking forward to seeing John again. Suddenly Steph had another pang of jealousy.

"You want to know who she is?" John smiled.

"Oh no, it's alright."

"Yes it is," said John putting his arms around Steph's neck. "Steph, I have had plenty of opportunities of going with other women; but frankly no one can live up to you, so stop worrying; and if you are that worried marry me now and come and live in Manchester."

"I'm just a bit nervous, all the women at the party are likely to be so glamorous and I'm just not in their league."

"No, you are way above it."

"Oh John, you know what I mean. They have the clothes and the figure."

"But you are just you and that means so much more to me. We can go and buy you a glamorous dress if you like."

"No I just wouldn't feel comfortable in it."

78

They walked to the local Indian. They had been there many times before but this time it seemed slightly different. It felt like there was something new and exciting about to happen.

"Do you think the public will like it?" John said.

"I don't know, what if they don't? What if I don't like it, what would you do then?"

"Have another go I suppose."

Steph wondered how he would react if it was a flop and began to realise that she had been so wrapped up in her own world that she really hadn't taken as much notice of John's as she should have done. He was entering a new world and trying to show the public part of her world. Didn't that, in fact, say it all about how much he loved her, that he had changed so much and yet she hadn't changed at all.

He had learnt to be patient and had the courage that she should have had to start to tell the public what social work was about. He had wanted a series but had managed to get the drama. It was the first step and whether it was a great success or an almighty failure he had tried and that was what mattered.

They walked back to the house and had ten minutes to spare before the programme.

Chapter Twenty-nine

Steph walked into the office nervously.

"It was fine, Steph," said Sarah encouragingly.

"No, it was awful," Steph replied. "It was just a way of getting a famous actress a bit of limelight. John's script and story were OK but it was the acting and filming that were awful."

"And how is John feeling?"

"Very low, he keeps saying that he has let me down. It is a week now and I'm really quite worried about him. He said that he couldn't understand why I wanted to be with him when he had let me down so badly."

Steph talked about the party and how most of the people there thought that it had been a success and there had been some good write-ups in the papers but John knew that the social work world would feel let down.

Steph went to see Ruby to talk about contact with Carly.

"I saw your guy's drama," she said. "So how's he feeling about it?"

"Rather low."

"Oh well, that's how things go. If he'd had our story it could have been a sensation," she said.

"But then nobody would believe that it was true, Ruby. Hollywood actresses don't beat their children up in Brummy hotels."

Steph had got to know Ruby well and liked her. She hated what she had done to Carly but she was getting to know the woman and the pressures that had driven her to do it. Ruby was paying a psychiatrist and psychologist to help sort her out. She said that she couldn't be back with Carly until she knew that she would never do anything like that again.

She had been a child actress but both of her parents, who in public seemed adoring, had beaten her on a regular basis. She had then attached herself to men with a similar kind of behaviour. She was recognising all of this but was very fearful that she might do something terrible again.

"Steph, I'm thinking of staying in the UK, what do you think?"

"What you mean? For good?"

"Yes, my grandparents on my dad's side were British and so I might have a chance, only they won't feel happy about what I have done to Carly and my agent won't be that happy, but Steph I have plenty of money so that side of things don't really matter. Carly and I don't need a mansion. I'd like to be a mum for a few years and drop the acting. What do you think?"

"Ruby, I just don't know you well enough; it might work, or you might get very frustrated. Why don't you just take each day at a time for now?"

"I don't want to keep living in a hotel and so I'm thinking of buying myself a little house. Where do you think is the best place to live in Birmingham?"

"Try Bournville, there are lots of lovely little parks there for Carly to play and the Selly Oak shops are an easy walk away or you could catch a bus."

"Yes it would be nice to walk, lots of people in the States never walk."

Everyone in the team seemed to be low again.

"What's going on?" said Steph, as she walked in after her visit to Ruby.

"It's Martin."

"What about Martin?" said Steph looking at the worried faces around her.

"He's taken an overdose and is in hospital."

"Oh shit," said Steph.

It didn't seem the right word but she was so shocked. Their rock had been crushed. Martin had always coped with everything, all the pressures that the team had been under and now he too had been defeated by those pressures.

"Can we go and see him?"

"Helen says that he can't cope with anyone at the moment."

Steph suddenly felt panic going through her system. They say that things always come in threes; well Steph was managing to pull herself together after the shock of Martin and her mobile rang. It was her sister ringing to say that their dad had had a massive heart attack and was in hospital. Steph just felt numb. Her three rocks were all vulnerable, all human.

Her beloved John was depressed, her rock of a boss was in despair and now her dad was teetering between life and death. Panic swept over her; she felt that she couldn't breath and went outside.

One of her old service users walked past the entrance of the office.

"Hi, Steph, guess what?"

"What?" said Steph in a rather disinterested way.

"I'm going to train to be a social worker."

Suddenly Steph found herself jolted from feeling sorry for herself.

"That's brilliant Daisy, well done."

Steph rang John.

"I'm going to marry you and come and live in Manchester," she said.

Chapter Thirty

The wedding was a quiet affair. Just close family and friends. Steph wanted to invite Ruby but Ruby understood why she couldn't. "You can't invite a child batterer to a social worker's wedding," she said. Steph didn't argue, it was just too important a day.

She had put John in charge of all of the arrangements and it had helped him get out of the doldrums.

Martin wasn't coping at all well. It seems that as well as the pressures of work he had found out that his wife Helen was having an affair with his supervisor, which, of course, led to numerous difficulties. Helen decided to leave Martin and so team members were not very happy about the situation.

But this was her big day and this time things were going to work. She had always had a thing about things working second time around and so this was a good omen.

John thought Steph looked beautiful in her pale pink silk dress. She looked just like a fairy princess. He had been so disappointed about the drama but when Steph had made the call to say she was coming to live in Manchester it had changed everything and now he just felt on top of the world.

They had decided to get married at Cadbury World. It had taken some arranging but it just seemed like the fun thing to do. They drove off to the airport in Blinky, John's Smart car. They were going to stay there that night before flying to Malaga the next day.

"Why don't you go somewhere exotic?" Lucy had said, but Steph said that it didn't really matter where they went.

Lucy giggled.

"You are a good one to talk," said Steph. Lucy was six months pregnant and looked stunning.

The flight to Malaga was on time and they descended the steps of the plane into bright sunshine. Steph felt slightly tipsy from the bottle of champagne that John had ordered on the plane.

"I'm just going to the loo," Steph said.

They collected their bags; of course, they got one fairly early on and had to wait ages for the second. They boarded the coach, which was nearly full, to take them to Nerja. They were staying in a hotel in the centre of Nerja and had asked for a sea view.

Steph looked out of the window and saw the barren countryside. There was so much building going on. She wondered how the Spaniards managed before the main road was built. She wondered how much more building could take place. She saw crops growing but there seemed to be nobody working.

She felt sleepy and leant on John. He put his arm around her. She felt so safe, so comfortable in her own personal bit of heaven and then she fell asleep.

It seemed like they were in another world as they ate their ice creams looking out to sea.

"When we are old can we live by the sea?" said Steph.

"Yes," said John, "that would be nice."

They decided to walk to the Nerja caves. It was a hot day and they had to stop several times to sip water from the bottles they had bought from the supermarket.

Steph couldn't decide whether she liked Nerja or not. "How can you like a place that is full of building sites?" she thought. But when they looked out to sea and breathed in the fresh sea air she felt heavenly. She knew that as long as John was not too far away she would be happy anywhere.

They arrived at the caves. They had been told how magnificent they were by a friend of John's who had visited them a few years before but Steph just felt in awe of their natural beauty. As they walked around they could see stories.

"It's like being in a cave full of fairy tales," said John who had brought along his digital camera and took shot after shot.

"Not sure how they will come out," he said.

"Never mind, that's the beauty of these cameras; you can ditch half of the pictures if they are crap," Steph said.

They decided to get a taxi back to the town, it was just so hot and suddenly Steph felt sleepy. They arrived at the hotel to find a new party of arrivals from the UK.

"I wish we'd booked two weeks," said John.

"Yes," said Steph, realising that they only had one more full day and then they would be packing up to go back home to their separate worlds.

Although they were married, they knew that it would be several months before Steph moved to Manchester. She couldn't just up and leave all her service users, some of whom depended on her. They had talked about this and Steph had agreed that she would give Martin three months' notice on her return.

Although the drama hadn't lived up to John or Steph's standards it had been well met by programme makers and had lead to some very interesting and well-paid work for John so it wouldn't matter if Steph didn't work for a while.

"Let's have a baby," John had said.

"We'll see what nature brings," said Steph.

They agreed not to use any contraceptives but as they made love in the hotel room Steph remembered the past and she began to fear that things just couldn't stay perfect for long.

Chapter Thirty-one

It was strange being back at work and going straight into a training session. Well, it wasn't really a training session, it was informing staff of ideas around the tracking system. Steph wasn't sure what she felt about the idea of tracking vulnerable children. She thought that the idea of having more formal links with health and education workers was a good idea but to track children who might need support from a formula seemed to be against a lot of social work principles about not labelling people.

"I think it reeks of the Gestapo," Tina, a social worker from another team, said cynically.

The trainer agreed but said that there wasn't a great deal that anyone could do about it.

"I don't agree," said Steph as she talked to John on the phone as she snuggled down for the night. "If only you media people would give us some air time we could debate such issues."

"So you are tired sweetie," said John, not commenting on Steph's last remark. He didn't want to get into an argument.

"What do you think then?" said Steph, not giving up on the discussion.

"I think that you are right but I can't take the responsibility for all of the media."

"I know, I am just tired, that's all… I wish you were here. It was so nice spending so much time with you… I miss you already."

"Time will go and you will be here with me and then you will be able to make your media contacts and influence the world. Now go to sleep, my love, and I'll talk to you tomorrow."

Steph didn't want to go but John persuaded her and said that he was only a phone call away. She snuggled down and the next thing she knew was that she was in a dream.

John was way out to sea on a little fishing boat. She knew he was there but she couldn't see or get to him. There were lots of people all around her and they were whispering different things to her. She decided to walk away from them and walked along a beach but, although the dream had started in Spain, this beach was somewhere else and she didn't know where it was. She turned to the crowd and shouted, "You are wrong," and suddenly they all stopped and looked at her.

John was now at her side. She didn't know where he had come from. He told her to tell them the truth and then she woke up.

Her alarm was going off. She leant over and switched it off. She felt tired. She wanted to go back to sleep to find out what happened next and cursed the alarm for waking her.

"Your Dad isn't feeling very well," said Steph's mum, "and so I've called the doctor."

"I'll just pop in and see him before I go to work then," said Steph.

Dad was pleased to see her and gave her a hug.

"Must go," said Steph, "I've got a case conference at 9.30 and need to get myself prepared."

Steph texted John to say that her Dad wasn't feeling very well. He replied that he hoped that he would be better soon. Steph thought no more of it and drove into work. She put the radio on in the car and the DJ was talking about the dream he had last night. It was uncanny because it was the same dream that Steph had had.

As soon as she had taken her coat off she rang her mum to ask how her dad was.

"He's fine," she said.

Steph felt pleased, she could get on with the day.

The conference was a tough one. It concerned a young baby with a mum who had been in care since she was a child. Both parents loved the baby but they just couldn't get on and when the mum was on her own she just didn't have the right skills to care for the baby. During the conference the parents started fighting and the police had to be called.

Steph had a strange feeling all day. She rang John to tell him to be careful driving and then later in the day she heard the news to say that there had been a fatality on the M6 and that the family had been informed. Steph couldn't believe it when she heard the name. It was Luke. She had forgotten all about him, but by the description it had to be him. That night she got home fairly early and watched the local news and sure enough there was a picture of Luke.

"Steph, I've got some great news," John said.

"What's that?" said Steph, trying to fight back her tears.

"What's up?" said John. He always knew when there was something wrong with Steph.

"Remember Luke?" she said but didn't leave him long enough to answer, "well, he's been killed."

"How?" said John.

"In a car accident on the M6."

John was quiet at the end of the phone. They talked about Luke and other day to day things and Steph then asked John what it was that he wanted to tell her.

"Never mind," he said, "I'll tell you another day."

Steph went to bed feeling sad. She had liked Luke, she knew he was wrong for her but she was so sad that she might never bump into him again. She sat next to her dad on the settee and gave him a nice cuddle.

"You know Dad," she said, "I really love you"

"I know," he said, "and I'm so lucky but it's time that you moved out and went to live with that fabulous husband of yours. You can change the world just as well in Manchester as you can here, you know."

"I know, Dad." She suddenly realised that yet again she had put herself first. John had been bursting to tell her something and she had spoilt it.

"What was your news?" she asked John when she made her bedtime call.

"Go to sleep Steph, its late, I'll tell you tomorrow."

But when the next day came she forgot to ask and he didn't tell her.

Chapter Thirty-two

"I'm getting a divorce," said Martin, when everyone was asked in the team meeting how they were.

No one knew what to say but Sue, who was sitting next to Martin, gave him a hug, which he responded to.

"They are both leaving," Martin said, referring to his wife and boss.

They had a visitor coming to the team meeting and so there was no more discussion. The team were close and knew each other well and so when one of them felt deep sadness it often impacted on the others, not to the extent that they became dysfunctional but often team members seemed to be quiet and contemplative as if they were waiting for something to happen to each of them.

"So, Steph, when are you going to Manchester?" Sarah asked.

"In about six weeks' time," she replied quietly.

"I saw your hubby on the TV the other night talking about his new project; it sounds very exciting."

Steph felt herself blushing, she knew nothing about John's knew project and began to panic in case she was quizzed on it but fortunately she was saved by the visitor to the team, who led a lively discussion on adoption which lifted the team spirit.

John was the most important person in her life and yet she had been selfish and put herself first. How could she hear from a colleague about her husband's exciting project and not know herself? She thought back to the night that she had heard about Luke's death and how John had said that he had exciting news. That was several weeks ago. She felt like a selfish fool.

She had been so caught up in herself and she knew that she loved John but it was him doing all the giving.

She had thought that social workers and journalists should try to understand each other better and so what had she done but married a journalist. One who had changed so much and who had come to realise why she was so passionate about her work. He had tried his hardest and was so disappointed with the social work response to the TV drama. But how could he know without her giving him the knowledge. She had been so wrapped up in her own world that she hadn't seen that his level of love was so great that he wanted to be there to use the world that he knew to help her fight the social work cause. And even after all of this she had just taken him for granted. Whenever she got herself in a state he had come rushing down from Manchester just to be with her and now she knew that she had to be there with him. She wanted to be a proper wife. Hearing these words made her cringe but it was true. She wanted to be by his side and she wanted another chance to be a mum and she knew that he so much wanted to be a dad too.

"I love you," she texted and immediately a reply came back saying that he loved her too, followed by eight kisses. She always sent him seven and she felt reassured when he sent her one more.

She planned to work at home that morning to try to catch up and so had brought three files home with her. She gazed at the files and thought of how much time she had spent with these families. She would miss them but she knew that it was time to move on.

She wasn't Stephanie Clover any more. She had always liked her name and had retained it at work when she had married Alan but now she felt different. She wanted to be Mrs Snow. It had a nice sound to it. Stephanie Snow. She practised signing her name on a piece of paper and found herself in a daydream where everything was perfect. But then she was startled by the phone ringing. She answered it, it was Sarah from work.

"Steph we need you at work. We need a video-trained social worker this afternoon."

"Why, what's happened?" said Steph, a bit irritated by the demand being put upon her.

"Its Mandy Jones; she absconded from Greystoke with Linda, who is only twelve years old, and they are both believed to have had sex with some men that Mandy met at a pizza place."

"OK, what time?"

"The police want you to be at the suite by four o'clock."

Steph thought about Mandy. She was fourteen years old and had been known to the team for about eighteen months; in that time she had to and fro, in and out of the care system. Her parents were quite well off but Mandy was just completely out of control. She had been to see all sorts of therapists but none of them seemed to be able to make her see how destructive her behaviour was. Her parents were either very supportive of her or rejecting of her. They would cooperate with individual social workers and then take Mandy back home saying that they didn't need any help any more, only to find a few weeks later that Mandy would return yet again to the care system.

She had been in three residential units and four foster homes. She had been to see psychiatrists and psychologists but no one seemed to be able to sort her out.

Both of her parents were GPs and were not short of money but Steph believed that this was part of their problem because when she went back home they would spoil her and after a few weeks when things were back to normal she would play up again.

Chapter Thirty-three

Steph was with Mandy's parents when her mobile rang.

"You'd better answer it," Gary Dinsdale said. "It might be something important."

"It's OK, it's my husband. I can ring him later."

Steph felt frustrated whenever she met the Dinsdales. They had two daughters, Sally who was in her first year at university and Mandy who was currently in the care system.

They loved them both equally but whereas Sally sailed through life being good at everything and achieving well, Mandy struggled with everything. She was dyslexic and from a very young age she had been difficult to manage both at home and at school.

"You spoilt her too much," said Steph.

"We know," Gary said, "but we can't go back in time."

"Mandy is very dramatic. Have you ever thought about her joining a youth theatre? Maybe she could direct her behaviour more positively in that environment."

"She did ballet when she was little but wasn't very keen on it."

"I bet the Rep have a youth theatre."

Steph left the Dinsdales thinking about it. It didn't stop her personal feelings of inadequacy.

She rang John before starting off back to the office.

"Have you got your diary?" John said.

"Yes."

"Well, block 22nd June in your diary."

"Why?"

"I've been nominated for an award for the drama and I want you to be there with me."

John sounded so excited; 22nd June was a week before she moved to Manchester and so Steph worried that she might have too much work to do.

"Steph, you must go. Whatever you have is not more important than being with John," said Lucy when she reached the office and told her.

Steph knew that Lucy was right. She began to realise that her life was changing. She would no longer be just a social worker, she was the wife of a journalist and as such would be entering a new world.

She began to feel sad about the people she was leaving behind but she had to move on. She remembered how uncertain she had been even right up to getting married to Alan but now she knew that not only was John the husband that she and many women sought but he was also her best friend.

He understood her and she needed to understand him more. They hadn't really talked about having kids but she knew that was what John wanted and she wanted it to work this time. She had been given her second chance.

"Wake up, dreamy," said Dad.

"Oh sorry Dad, I was miles away."

"Your mum and I were saying that if it was OK with you and John we'd like to come and stay for a few days in August and then we could catch a train to see your Auntie Eileen in Edinburgh."

"You should feel free to come whenever you like."

"I know love, but you and John need some settling in time, you've had rather a strange start to a marriage, living in different cities."

"Yes, but hopefully we've got plenty of years together and I was glad I was here while you were ill, Dad. You gave me and Mum a couple of nasty frights."

"Well, when your times up there's not much you can do about it … oh sorry love I didn't mean to…"

Steph knew that her Dad felt uncomfortable but she couldn't cry forever about Alan and she had moved on in life. Other people weren't as fortunate as her she had worked with several families where deaths in the family had led to them being permanently split up.

At times she had thought that she would fall apart too but she just had the survival instinct and now she had so much to live for.

"John's on the phone," said Mum, passing the handset to Steph.

"Put Channel 4 on at 11pm," said John in an excited voice.

He told her that they were going to review a programme which he had been heavily involved in; she remembered him telling her about it at the time but the night it was on there had been a crisis at work and so she didn't get home in time. This seemed to be the story of her life. "I must be more attentive," she thought. Everyone thought that she was a caring, giving person but was she when she kept putting her work before her husband? What would she do if she had kids? Would they be out on the street while she attended to somebody else's kids?

She began to panic.

"You're drifting off again," said Dad. "Why don't you go to bed?"

"I've got to watch the review of John's programme."

"Well, we're off," said Mum.

It was 10.30pm and Steph wondered if she could stay wake.

The programme started and she found herself dozing through the monotone voice of the presenter. She awoke to be faced by her husband.

"And where did you get your inspiration from?" said the presenter.

"My wife," John said. "She is a social worker."

Steph sat bolt upright. John was on national TV talking about her and she had nearly slept through it.

They showed an extract from the programme which was a documentary about people who had survived a murder in their family. She listened to a man saying what he had felt towards the murderers and she thought that she hadn't even dealt with this. Tears ran down her cheeks. She just didn't know how she felt and suddenly she felt anger towards John. How could he make a programme that was so close to what she had experienced?

She felt that his journalist roots had betrayed her. She had been put in a gold fish bowl and she felt so vulnerable. What had she done marrying such a man?

Chapter Thirty-four

"You didn't tell me that you would be on," she said.

"What's wrong?" John said, sounding confused.

"It's my story, John. How could you betray me? What was it for? Good TV?"

Steph found herself screaming down the phone at John and then when she hung up she felt so guilty.

She had a restless night and wanted to ring John; several times she started dialling his number. At 6am she fell into a deep sleep but was suddenly awoken by the sound of the doorbell. She looked at the clock, it was 8.20.

She leapt out of bed thinking she must have slept through her alarm. She heard noises and wondered who was visiting at this early hour.

"John has driven through the night to see you," Mum said in an annoyed tone. "He seems very upset."

"Where is he?"

"In the living room. I've got to get to work … Your dad has already gone … be nice to him."

Mum started fussing. Steph knew how much both of her parents liked John and she knew that she was wrong. He just hadn't understood, that's all. The programme had just stirred up memories.

She opened the living room door and saw a very worried John.

"I'm so sorry," he said, sitting motionless on the settee.

"No, it's my fault … I seem to have become so selfish. I didn't even see the whole programme. I'd wanted social work to become more high profile and remember telling you that you could use my own story if it helped … but I just didn't realise how much it would hurt … to have those reminders … you must hate me."

"Of course I don't, I love you … it's just that sometimes I don't understand you and, yes, I feel left out. You fight the causes of your service users and yet seem to be in some kind of dream world when I tell you things. Most of the time I don't mind but occasionally it just gets to me, that's all."

Steph sat on the settee and soon she felt comfortable in John's arms.

"I'll be in later," she said to Dawn the receptionist. "About one o'clock I should think."

And she snuggled down next to the person who just meant so much to her.

It was nearer to two when Steph got to the office. She gathered all the messages out of her pigeon hole and amongst all the paperwork was a note saying that she should attend the funding panel for Mandy Dinsdale at 10am on 22nd June.

"Oh no," she groaned.

"What's up?" said Mark.

"Oh nothing," Steph replied.

But it was far from nothing, for a second she panicked. She had promised John that she would go to his award ceremony.

"Oh shit," she said aloud, not realising that Martin was standing nearby.

"Charming," he said. "What's up?"

She told him about the award ceremony.

"How exciting. So our Steph is entering a whole new world."

"But what about the panel?"

"What's the problem? You can get a train straight afterwards and be there in plenty of time."

"Of course I could," she thought. Why was she panicking? Perhaps it was the whole idea of going to such a thing. She wouldn't know what to say to people, it would just be too alien to her.

She thought about the panel. It was so important for her to be there. Mandy was such a needy young person and, although she liked her parents, they just could not cope with her.

They had found out that she had been abused for years by her father's cousin and at the time had been devastated. It had split the once close-knit family in two. One half of the family supported her and the other side thought that she was making the whole thing up and when the cousin was sent to prison they were livid.

At one time they had eight children from the same family being looked after because of concerns surrounding the cousin. All except for Mandy had been returned to their homes.

Steph had been attending panels on and off for two years; she would get a new out-of-county placement for Mandy but after a short period it would always break down. She had now found a placement that seemed much more suitable for her needs but it was going to cost a hefty £3,750 per week.

Lucy said that if the public knew how much some of these private children's homes cost they would be flabbergasted. OK, some of them had staff on a one-to-one basis and claimed to have therapeutic input but when social workers got their kids placed they often felt that the care didn't live up to what was offered.

Steph had spent some time checking this particular home out and at £3,750 a week it still seemed expensive but the staff were a mixture of health and social work trained with the owner being a psychotherapist who seemed very committed to change.

Mandy had run off so many times and had over the last year had sex with several men of all ages. She just had such low self esteem and had written letters to Steph and her parents declaring that there was just no point in living.

Chapter Thirty-five

It was Carly's fourth birthday and Steph was invited to the party at the foster parents' house.

"How are you?" said Ruby looking stunning in a long flowing, tight-fitting, crimson-coloured dress. "How's married life?"

"Rather strange," said Steph.

She told Ruby how John was living in Manchester.

"What are you doing here girl when you've got a guy like him?"

Steph made some kind of reply but it sounded rather weak. She realised that although she was excited at the prospect of going to Manchester she was also a little scared.

"You're looking a bit peeky," June, the foster parent, said as she brought out another jug of orange squash. "They're a thirsty bunch."

"June, you are a marvel," Ruby exclaimed not giving Steph time to comment but then she didn't really want to anyhow.

Steph knew that Ruby and June got on like a house on fire but she also felt that it was time that Ruby and Carly started being back together. She had said this to Ruby at the recent review but Ruby had said that she was still frightened of what she might do. Steph wondered whether Ruby would keep saying this. She was a charming woman and she enjoyed her company but was it also convenient for her?

"You are looking peeky," said Mum.

"I'm just a bit tired," said Steph.

"Well I hope you're not coming down with something just before John's big night; that would be typical of you."

"What do you mean?"

"Well, every time that John has had something important happen you have been too busy with your work. He's your husband now. You really should be putting him first."

"That's rather an old-fashioned attitude, love," said Dad from behind the Evening Mail.

"It's true though. John has stuck by Steph through all those bad patches in her life and loves her to pieces but in return …"

"In return she loves him too," said Dad dropping his paper and coming to give Mum a hug. "Just like I love you and put up with your quirks."

As Steph went to her room she left her parents debating the rights and wrongs of the universe. She was tired but also nervous about going to the award ceremony. She just felt that she wouldn't fit in. She had talked to John briefly but decided to have an early night.

John felt that there was something wrong. Steph sounded different to usual. She said that she was going to have an early night. He decided to have a go at his novel but he felt restless.

He went for a walk and, passing the Fox and Hounds, he saw a group of young men and women in an inebriated state and remembered what he had been like when he was younger. He had been a Jack the lad and had had so many conquests in his time.

He had no regrets about marrying Steph. He knew that she was the right woman for him but he just wanted her around all the time, not just some of the time. He just hated coming home these days to an empty house.

The air was fresh and it settled him. He decided to head back home; he suddenly found that the ideas were flowing and he wanted to get them down while they were still there. He walked into the quiet house, kicked his shoes off in the hall, went to the kitchen to make a coffee and then settled at his computer in the spare room.

"Chapter Sixteen," he wrote.

"As I walked the streets late at night ..." And then the whole story flooded in front of him.

Steph was woken by the alarm. She had slept like a baby.

"How are you this morning?" said Mum as she washed up her breakfast dishes.

"Fine. Why don't you use the dishwasher, Mum?"

"I suppose habits just die hard," she replied.

John woke with a stiff neck, he looked at the clock it was 6.30am. He had planned to wake at 7am.

"Oh shit," he said aloud to the empty room.

He had an important meeting and he had fallen asleep on the chair by his computer.

He looked, bleary eyed, at the screen and whizzed back remembering that he had started at Chapter Sixteen. He had written nineteen pages.

"I expect its all crap," he thought, but he knew that he had no time now to read it and appraise his own creativeness. He must shower and get ready to go to his meeting.

This meeting could make a whole difference to his life.

Chapter Thirty-six

It was 9.30am and a call came through for Steph.

"Can I ring them back?" Steph said to Eileen, one of the receptionists. "I have to go to the funding panel."

Steph jotted a note to ring the children's unit when she returned.

As she signed herself out a text arrived on her mobile. She got her mobile out of her bag. It was from John and was wishing her luck.

"Love you," it ended.

"Love you too," Steph thought, suddenly feeling a little dizzy.

"Are you OK?" said Eileen.

"I'll be fine when I get out into the fresh air."

Steph sat in the reception of headquarters waiting for her turn. It felt like she was waiting for a job interview. Paul came down the stairs. He knew Steph well from the number of times that she had come to the funding panel and had said many times over the phone that he and the social workers could only do their jobs to the best of their ability.

Steph picked up a leaflet which told the public about the new law on smacking. "How ridiculous," Steph thought.

"Well, how did you get on?" said Martin.

"What do you think?" said Steph, looking disheartened.

"We'll just have to think of something else."

Steph understood why the panel was reluctant to give the funding, at £3,750 a week. Steph would also feel the same but sometimes the frustration of what to do with so many of these young people was unbearable. The government just appeared to be clueless.

She rang the children's unit to find that Jamie had absconded for the third night in a row. Yet again he had gone back home and had been returned by the police. The police were calling for a strategy meeting but what could she do? Jamie loved his mum and dad but they just couldn't manage him. At fourteen he was a big lad in fact; he towered above both of his parents and although at times his behaviour was OK, at others he was so unpredictable and had trashed both his bedroom and the living room.

"We just can't manage him," Susan Crowe (his mother) had said through a flood of tears.

At the time Steph wanted to cry too but later had vented her frustration in the team meeting.

But today she was going off to be with her man. She had done what she could and had forceably given her view at the funding panel. She had managed to get an extra worker to work specifically with Jamie but this still felt only like a plaster job.

She caught the train to Manchester and suddenly realised that she was about to enter a whole new world as the wife of a successful journalist. She suddenly felt sick and as the train pulled out of New Street station she stuck her head out but instead of a blast of fresh air she smelt stale fumes.

"Oh bugger, my dress is all screwed up," said Steph.

"There's plenty of time until we need to go."

"I need a snooze, I feel knackered."

"Well, I can have a go at ironing it, but you know that I'm not that good."

"Practice makes perfect," Steph said, curling her arm around John's neck in the way he so loved. "Second thoughts, leave it, I'll do it."

She lay on their bed and drifted off to the sound of children at the local school as they were being met from school by their parents. It was a comforting sound. It was so nice to hear happy voices. So much of her work was concerned with unhappy situations that sometimes she couldn't believe that there were families that could cope on their own.

But then she had. She had got through Steve leaving. Had trained and become a successful social worker. Had coped with Alan and Paul's deaths.

She had survived and knew that many people survived. She had glimpsed periods of happiness through her gloom.

And yes, her mum was right, she now needed to put John first. He had always been there for her and when she was with him she felt happy and contented and, in fact, the last few times she had been to Manchester she hadn't wanted to go back to Birmingham. She knew that once she was there permanently she could start the next bit of her life.

She had been so impatient; it was John that had been courageous.

He had looked at how he used to be and had changed and he had tried to fight for more coverage of social work but, without her, he could only tell stories, not feel them. She had so much that she wanted to say about what she was feeling, in particular concerning one issue.

"Should I tell John before or after the award ceremony tonight?" she thought.

She decided to consult her runes.

John thought that she was nutty, but so many times the runes had been right. John said that they were written in such a way that you could read anything into them but Steph felt that there were distinctly positive and negative runes and one that described freezing your action.

She fell into a deep sleep and forgot all about the runes.

"Time to wake up sweetheart," said John, gently kissing her.

He lay down on the bed next to her and she snuggled up to him.

"I've got something to tell you," she said.

Chapter Thirty-seven

"I hope it's something nice," said John.

The phone rang and John picked it up.

"It's your mum," said John passing the phone to Steph.

"I just wanted to remind you what I said about John," she said. "I know what your dad said but I think I'm right, you should put him first."

"Yes, Mum, you were right," Steph said. "I'll ring you tomorrow and let you know how it went. I need to go now."

"You were going to tell me something," John said as Steph handed him back the receiver to put on the base.

"Oh, it's nothing," she said trying to play it down.

"As long as you are happy, that's all that matters," John commented. "Oh, and I know you said that I shouldn't but I've ironed your dress."

Steph had been to the toilet six times in the last half an hour. She just felt so nervous.

"Are you sure that I look alright?" said Steph for the third time.

"Yes, you look lovely," John said.

He was so patient with her, she tried to relax but panic came over her. She went into the back garden and took some deep breaths. It was a warm June evening. "What a magical date," she thought. The day after Midsummer's Day.

"The car's here," said John.

Of course, it wasn't a car it was a limousine. The TV company wanted the nominees to arrive in style. "Just pretend that you are a Hollywood film star," whispered George, the driver, who was obviously used to nervous up-and-coming stars.

She felt a little better and sat next to John in the back seat. They were the first to be picked up and the driver set off to pick up three other nominees and their partners. They stopped at the first house and a rather ugly looking man and a not so good looking woman stepped into the car. This was Tom, a sound engineer, and his wife.

"Is this your first time?" she said to Steph.

"Yes."

"Tom has been to loads of these things, he always seems to get nominated but then a younger better looking person gets the award. We really just go along these days for a free meal and a night out from the kids."

Steph laughed; she liked this woman and found out later that she too was called Steph.

She began to relax. The next house was rather grander than Tom and Steph's.

"Who are we picking up from here?" Steph said to the other Steph.

"A presenter who used to be a footballer for a team in the third division, wasn't it Tom?"

"Something like that I think," said Tom who was not particularly interested.

"His wife is about twenty years younger than him and aspires to have her own show. He's actually quite nice but she well …"

Steph thought this was ominous and she found that she was beginning to enjoy herself.

"Are you alright, love?" said John, cuddling Steph.

"Absolutely fine," she said.

Getting out of the limousine was fun and Steph found herself getting excited.

The ex-footballer's wife posed for the cameras in her very revealing dress and Steph felt rather frumpy in comparison.

The third couple were much older. He was a producer who had worked for the TV company for thirty years and his wife was a few years older than him.

She walked next to Steph as they entered the theatre where the award ceremony was taking place.

"A lot of it's pretty superficial you know," she said.

Steph found herself sitting next to this woman, who introduced herself as Pauline. Her husband Clive seemed to have an intense discussion with John.

"So you know John well?" quizzed Steph.

"Not that well," Pauline replied, "but Clive has mentioned him … he says that he has quite a few original and interesting ideas."

Steph suddenly felt a little queasy.

"I just need to pop to the loo," she said to Pauline.

Steph just made it in time and threw up down the loo. She just had to tell John otherwise someone else would. She had now done three tests and they had all proved positive. It wasn't that she didn't want another baby … it was just …

"Are you alright?" said Pauline. "You seemed to rush off rather."

"Just nerves I suppose," Steph said lying.

"We're popping out for a fag," Clive said. "Are you coming?"

"I gave up," said John.

"OK. There will be a break for half an hour, then they will go live," Clive said.

"Are you alright sweetheart?" said John, looking rather concerned. "I've got something to tell you," he said excitedly.

"And I've got something to tell you," said Steph.

"You go first," he said.

"No you."

"OK," he said with an even more excited look on his face.

"I've got my own chat show."

"Wow." Steph didn't know what else to say.

"How often?" she said.

"Twice a week at 10.30pm."

"Wow."

"Is that all you can say?" John said smiling.

"Wow, wow, wow," she said hugging John closely to her and showering him with kisses.

"So what's your news?" he said.

Steph suddenly felt nervous and her world went flashing by.

"I…" she said nervously.

"Look, for once there is no one here to interrupt us."

"Yes," she said, "I…"

"You what?" he said, becoming a little impatient with her.

Suddenly it all came tumbling out.

"Oh that's fabulous," said John.

"What's fabulous," said Pauline wafting the smell of smoke over them.

"We're having a baby."

"I thought as much," said Pauline, winking at Steph.

Steph knew that Pauline knew because of her rushed trip to the toilet and she felt so relieved that she had told John. She had wanted to tell him for weeks but it was just never the right time and, as he said, there was always an interruption.

The rest of the evening seemed to float by. John was so excited Steph would soon be living with him full time. He was going to start the chat show in three weeks' time and he was going to be a dad. He just wanted to grin so much and then he heard his award being announced.

"The prize for the most original screenplay goes to …"

Chapter Thirty-eight

"You can't have everything," Steph said.

But she knew how disappointed John was and to give an award to yet another cop drama was just ludicrous.

"How could they think that that was more original?" she said to Lucy as she spoke on the phone. "John is over the moon about the baby. And have I told you about his chat show?"

"Perhaps he'll give up the writing and concentrate on that then," Lucy said.

"I shouldn't think so, it's in his blood and he's still writing the novel but won't show me any of it."

"What's it called?"

"I don't know? In fact, I don't think that he's got a title for it yet."

"Got to go, see you at your do on Thursday."

"Ok," said Steph.

Only two days away and she had so much to do before she left on Friday. How would she get it all done in time. Each farewell visit made her feel weepy.

Katie Jones, whose daughter Daisy was fostered and who Steph had had a difficult time with, thrust a box of chocolates in her face.

"I know we've had our run-ins, Steph, but 'ere, 'ave this … go on."

Steph didn't know what to say; she felt choked up inside.

"Well, if you've won Katie Jones over, you can win anyone," said Martin as he scoffed a chocolate out of the box.

Thursday morning came and Steph had call after call wishing her well.

"Don't forget us," said Jane from Finance.

"Wow," said Steph to John.

"Seems to be your favourite word at the mo. Shall we call our kid Wow and then you can use it all the time?"

"If you were here you know what would happen."

"That's how little Wow started her journey," John said, giggling down the phone. "You know, Steph, it is gonna be so strange not talking to you on the phone. I have done it for so long that it's just part of me and, well, I shall have to start having more baths."

"What do you mean?" she said. "You mean that you go to work stinking?"

"Got you," he said.

John was a wonderful prankster; he loved to stir Steph up and she spent so much time laughing at some of the things that he came out with

104

"Oh you ..." she said.

That "Oh you" resounded through John's head and he wrote it in Chapter Thirty-three. The novel was coming on and now he had the title. He had been stumped for names but he knew that it could only be one thing and that was Wow.

As he typed those three letters he just knew that this time it would work. He was always nearly there but this time they would realise that what he was writing was worth first prize. He sipped his coffee, nibbled his shortbread and entered his world that belonged to him alone.

Steph's leaving do was nice and packed with people. The food looked gorgeous spread in front of her. The speech had been made and now it was her turn.

"Wow," she said and then giggled. "Well, it's fab seeing so many people and I'm going to miss you all and thank you so much for the presents. I have loved working with all of you but am looking forward to my new life in Manchester and, well, actually I have some other news." Steph hesitated as she said this. "I'm having a baby."

The response was amazing and Steph was showered with hugs and smiles everyone was so pleased for her. She nibbled at a carrot.

"Well, you should make the most of the puddings while you can," said Sue the clerk, who was always on some weird and wonderful diet. "I put three stone on with my first."

These words stuck in her head. "This isn't my first," Steph thought and a flash memory reminded her of that awful night when Steve had lost his first.

But that was a long time ago and she knew that this time it would all go well. She had survived and come through.

"Will you get a social work job in Manchester?" Derek the area manager asked.

"I'm not sure yet," Steph replied. "I just want to chill out for a bit and get used to my new life. John has got his own chat show and so, with his writing, we won't be short of money."

"But you won't give it up forever, will you Steph?" Derek said. "We need people like you."

Steph went home that night with those words in her head but she didn't really know what she wanted to do. She knew that she could probably stay at home for the rest of her life but that just didn't feel right.

Chapter Thirty-nine

"Moss Side is just not a good place to bring up a baby," said John's mum as Steph sat in their caravan.

They had stayed for a few days but now she was feeling ready to go home.

"She's right," said John's dad, "and now that John is earning more, why don't you move?"

"I was going to suggest that we look for something new but had a more radical idea," said John.

"I know that Steph misses being near to her mum and, now that her dad is not too well again, I thought ..."

"I don't want to move back to Birmingham," Steph interrupted.

"I wasn't thinking of that but what about somewhere in between Manchester and Brum, perhaps a village? I think it would be nice to live in a village."

Steph was five months pregnant and could not think of moving. It was six weeks since she had finished work and she was still enjoying the novelty of being at home.

"Don't you miss social work?" John had quizzed her a few times but she could honestly say that she didn't; besides the scan showed that they were, in fact, going to have twins and she knew that she would be busier with two and that it would be more difficult to get a childminder but for now she had no intention of even thinking about it. Strangely she liked being dependent on John and she enjoyed watching him on his chat show. He was still freelancing a bit and writing his novel and so he seemed very happy.

She liked nesting, as one of her new friends called it. Some of the women at the antenatal clinic were a bit like some of the women that she had had on her caseload and, in fact, talked about their social workers but they didn't know that she had so recently been a social worker and she decided to keep it that way.

She ignored John's comment and just carried on with her daily tasks and enjoyed reading some of the books that she had collected over the years and never opened.

Shortly after her move to Manchester she had had a memorable weekend as John had taken her to the Jane Austen Society AGM. He had kept up his avid interest and wanted to go so Steph agreed to tag along.

The AGMs took place at Chawton where Jane Austen had lived until she moved to Winchester just before she died. They had booked a B and B about half an hour away for two nights and had decided that on the Sunday they would go to Stonehenge and then Steventon, where Jane Austen was born and lived until she was twenty-five, before they headed back to Oxford, where they had booked another night.

They arrived at the B and B at 6pm and Steph felt very tired as it was a long drive from Manchester. The kingsize bed felt very comfy and Steph drifted off into a nice sleep.

John had brought his laptop with him and when Steph awoke she saw him avidly writing.

"What's the time?" she said in a croaky voice.

"Ten to eight."

"Oh, I've been asleep for ages," she croaked.

"Well, I've written six pages since you've been asleep but haven't looked back at them to see if they are any good."

"Let me look," she said, leaning towards John.

"No," he said forcefully, "not until I've finished."

"But when will that be?" said Steph in a whiney voice.

"Dunno," was all the reply that she got.

Steph was intrigued but she knew that she had to be patient. John had had several disappointments and so he had to do this at his own pace. She had noticed that recently he had the bug for writing.

"I wish I was like Jane Austen," John whispered, as they listened to the academic talking about imminent and planned writers.

"But surely most people are somewhere in the middle," Steph said.

"I suppose so but perhaps, because I've been a journalist, I have to plan things more. I do sometimes get flows of inspiration when the story just comes out and I'm amazed when I read back to see that it just makes sense."

"I love you as you are," said Steph, snuggling closer to John but she also knew that he wouldn't be completely contented until he had that one book that made sense.

John thought about what Steph said as he waited for her to return from the portable toilets; most of the time he was very happy but she couldn't know how he felt, that he just wanted that one book, that one that just made sense. He would then be completely happy.

Steph had expected the people at the AGM to dress up a bit; they all seemed a bit drab in their neutral-coloured clothing. She had worn a sky blue coloured dress which flowed in the breeze.

"The weather's not so good today," said a man standing next to her in the tea queue. "Do you know, I have been coming to the AGM meetings for over twenty years and the whole of that time it has always been beautiful sunny days but its threatening a bit today."

The morning had been the AGM business and the afternoon was the academic. In the middle they had sat under an old oak tree and eaten their picnic of tiger bread and cheese.

"Asda's tiger bread tastes a bit better than this one," Steph said.

John was amused.

He liked this; being here it made him feel at home even though nearby was a car park full of cars with people coming from all over the country to pay homage to this quiet unassuming woman who had just written because she liked writing. He wondered what she would think of all of this.

"By what you've told me about Jane Austen," said Steph, "she wouldn't like all of this homage."

"No, probably not," said John, dozing in the brief glimpses of sunshine, wondering how Steph could be thinking exactly the same as him.

Steph looked at John and thought that he really was a woman's dream, being a cross between Mr Darcy and Mr Knightley; in fact, when she first knew him he could have also been some of the baddie characters in Jane Austen books which she couldn't remember the names of. It had been years since she had read any of them and was intrigued by John's interest. She would have thought that he would be more interested in the writings of Charles Dickens but she knew that there was just something about the Austen stories that had brought out his gentler side and she liked it.

The meal at the pub across the road from the B and B was OK but they both agreed that they had had much better.

The breakfast was good but Steph decided not to eat the eggs although she loved them and was given a second sausage instead.

"When's the baby due?" said the woman who owned the B and B.

"Mid-November," Steph and John chorused.

The woman was amused by them both replying at the same time.

"And we are having twins," John said proudly.

"Double trouble then," the woman laughed.

The trip to Stonehenge was short and as they arrived it seemed as though the whole world was arriving too. They listened to the commentary as they walked around and the male voice telling them about the stones sounded familiar but when Steph asked John, he didn't know who it was.

"Everyone looks so peaceful," said John as he watched people walking around.

"Yes and I am too," she said. "I like bringing the twins here and I think we should come back with them when they are two."

"OK," he said, smiling at Steph.

He could see that she was making plans.

"And will they have a little sister on the way by then?" he said smiling.

"Who knows? It'll probably depend on whether they are little angels or brats, don't you think? Besides stop wishing my life away," Steph said, poking John in the ribs.

"It would be nice to come here later in the season and see the sunset," John said.

"Yes, I imagine that sometimes it is spectacular and when they have built the tunnel so you can look across the fields it will be even more so."

Steph felt entranced by the place and understood why it had so much regard in the world; there was just something vibrant and magical about it, it wasn't just a pile of old stones.

They walked back to the car and headed on to Steventon.

Chapter Forty

"How sad," said John.

"Yes," Steph replied rubbing his back gently.

John was slightly upset; the grandeur of Chawton towered above Steventon. All that remained of the Jane Austen family was a pump in a field. This had apparently been in the house that Jane had been born in and lived in until she was twenty-five.

"How come nobody has bought the field or done anything with it?" Steph said.

"Perhaps the farmer won't sell it," John said.

Barbed wire surrounded the field and the pump was surrounded by overgrown vegetation.

"Well, when you have your bestseller you should meet with the farmer and see if you can do a deal to buy some of the field," Steph said.

"You should be the writer," John said, "you have such dreams and aspirations."

"But I can't get them on paper like you, I don't know how some of these writers sit for hours on end writing. I would just get so bored and feel completely guilty about all the jobs that I had to do."

John laughed.

"Perhaps they have cooks and cleaners to do them for them."

"Its still sad though," said Steph as they walked back to the car.

The rain that had been hanging around suddenly came and for a while John had to put the wipers on full speed.

"We won't get in the Smart car for much longer," he said.

"You can still use it for work," Steph said. "But perhaps we should get a new car, mine is a bit unreliable these days."

"Yes, I'll get some advice off Pete."

John's friend Pete knew a lot about cars and John was averse to buying new cars as he felt that they depreciated too quickly in value. But for today Steph wasn't interested, she was enjoying just being somewhere different, and so they headed off to Oxford.

It was about 4pm when they arrived in Oxford and they found their B and B. They decided to have a brief walk around the town. They had both been there before but not for many years.

"Its nice," said Steph as they ate a scone and drank hot chocolate, "but I wouldn't want to live here. Its too busy and full of tourists."

"Including us," said John laughing. "I remember a friend of mine who went to York University and he used to have a badge that said 'I am not a tourist I live here'."

"Perhaps that's why the locals in Steventon don't advertise that it's Jane Austen's birth place."

"Maybe, but it's still sad."

They had a lovely meal in an Italian restaurant but Steph refrained from drinking. She wasn't going to do anything to lose these babies, they meant so much to her.

As John brushed his teeth he could see Steph already in bed from the mirror.

He felt so contented; he had everything that he wanted and he wanted everything to just stay like this. He liked this sense of calm.

"So where were you thinking of us living?" said Steph as they snuggled down in bed.

"Perhaps a village near Stafford and then I could get a train easily to Manchester and you could get to Birmingham easily to see your mum and dad."

Steph had been disappointed that her parents' visit had been postponed because yet again her father wasn't very well.

"I'm fed up with this," he had told her at the time on the phone.

She had only just got to Manchester and John was on about moving. It had initially put her off but they had talked about buying a bigger house as two bedrooms wouldn't be enough and John was now earning a lot more money.

"We'll have to find a B and B near Stafford one day and go and explore," she said.

"So you're not against the idea then?" John said.

"As long as you don't keep moving us," she said. "I want to settle and make friends."

She had missed her friends from Birmingham and had thought about making some new friends but now she felt unsettled again.

"Let's just enjoy the rest of our break for now," she said.

"Yes," said John as he listened to Steph gently snoring next to him; to him it sounded like sweet purring.

Chapter Forty-one

"Oh, that guy is just impossible," John said as he arrived home from his late-night chat show. He was talking about the producer who had assured him that he would have a say in who came on his programme.

The show was successful, the public liked John but he was frustrated it was turning into just any old chat show; he had had ideas to make it different.

"Quit then," said Steph.

"I can't, the money's too good and with the babies..."

"I can always go back to work," Steph said.

"But I know that you don't want to; no I'll just have to last it out and look at the same time at different options. I could take up that offer of a column with the Reader but it wasn't the one I wanted. It's entertainment and you know that what I really want is social affairs."

"Never mind," Steph said, "it'll sort itself out." She knew that this was rather pathetic reassurance but she didn't know what else to offer as consolation at the moment. "Why don't you invite the producer and his wife over for a meal and perhaps we can try to plant some ideas into his head."

"That sounds a good idea."

"Just give me a couple of days' notice and try to find out what he likes to eat, we'll sweeten him up, you'll see."

John knew that if Steph put on the charm job she could nearly always get what she wanted and so he'd take the risk and put the producer in her hands.

"Invite another couple too so that it isn't so much in your face."

In the end John invited two other couples, Pete, his friend who found him good cars, and Cath and Carl, their elderly next door neighbours.

"What have you invited Pete for?" said Steph.

"I've heard that Bruce is interested in old cars and so…"

"I see," said Steph, interrupting, "you thought that Pete could help you win Bruce over."

"Something like that."

"But would Pete care who was on your show?"

"No but Helen, his latest girlfriend, would and, cor, she's a real looker."

"But won't that put Bruce's wife off?"

"With Pete around… no way."

Steph knew what John was saying as many women had fallen for the looks and charm of Pete. John had been surprised that Steph hadn't and had been a little wary of her meeting him at first but his topics of discussion generally bored Steph and often she would creep away to do something else when he called by. She was interested to see what the gorgeous Helen was like though, but for now she had to think of her latest antinatal appointment and their trip to Staffordshire.

She was also wondering whether she could do some social work just to keep her hand in.

"They are desperate for practice teachers," Lucy had said when she chatted about how things were going.

"But I'm moving probably."

"Where?"

"To somewhere near Stafford; John thinks that it would be easier as he only has to go to Manchester twice a week. Most of the time he works from home."

"Must be nice having him around. I wish I saw more of Tom but the job just gets worse and he seems to get all the kids who are placed miles from home. He's got one placed down in Dorset and has to stay overnight when he goes to visit."

Steph realised what a good life she had and, yes, she did like seeing a lot of John. But perhaps Lucy was right, what she should do was be a practice teacher and work with social work students for a few years, just to keep her hand in and to work around the twins.

She patted her tummy and spoke to the twins, "Mummy and Daddy are going to love you so much."

"Who are you talking to?" said John as he came in from the garden.

"The twins," she said.

"Oh, of course," he said, smiling.

Chapter Forty-two

"Bruce, this is my wife Steph," said John as he invited a rather large man, dressed in what Steph thought looked like a rather expensive pair of trousers and jacket, into the living room.

"And this is my wife Jackie," he replied.

They all shook hands and then John offered drinks.

The doorbell rang and Steph opened the door to Pete, Helen, Carl and Cath.

"Are they here yet?" said Cath.

"Yes," said Steph.

"So… what are they like?"

"I don't know, they've only just arrived and I haven't had a chance to get to know them yet."

They went into the living room and Jackie suddenly exclaimed.

"What was that about?" said John as he helped Steph get the dishes out of the oven.

"How do I know?"

They ate, but there seemed to be an awkwardness between Jackie and Pete.

Helen and Bruce got on like a house on fire and chatted about all sorts of things and in particular politics.

They dispersed while Bruce, Jackie, Cath and Carl went out to the garden for a smoke and Helen popped to the toilet and so with only John and Pete in the room Steph decided to find out the truth. What was there between Pete and Jackie.

"She's an old girlfriend," he said.

"Oh," said Steph thinking that she sounded just like Helen.

"We went out together for a couple of years and then she dumped me, that was years ago though."

"We have three children," said Bruce a while later after he and Pete had an intense discussion about the pros and cons of what, to Steph, seemed like an endless yawn of cars.

"We have two boys who belong to both of us and a girl who Jackie had before I knew her and is just as much my daughter."

Steph looked at John and he knew what she was thinking.

"Must be," said Steph as they stood in the kitchen making the coffee.

"No, far too much of a coincidence."

But when they went back into the living room they overheard Pete telling Bruce that Jackie used to be his girlfriend.

"When was it that we went out together?" said Pete to Jackie.

"I don't know," she said in a cagey way and immediately changed the subject to the chat show.

"Do you reckon what I reckon?" said Cath to Steph as she helped her load the dishwasher.

"Depends what it is," said Steph.

Cath and Carl were their next door neighbours and were very friendly but sometimes Steph wondered whether to discourage them from popping in so much as John worked at home. Most of the time when he was writing he could lock himself away but sometimes Cath would arrive just as he was making a coffee and then that was his writing for the day.

They were both in their seventies and retired and seemed to have plenty of time on their hands.

"Well, I reckon that Pete is the father of Jackie's kid."

"So do I," said Steph.

"But we better keep it hush hush."

"Got any After Eights?" said Carl, coming into the kitchen.

"Steph's not that posh," said Cath.

Steph laughed at the idea of After Eights being posh.

"You should get a few ordinary people on your programme John," said Helen sitting next to and flirting with Bruce.

"We get bored with all those silly girls with their tits hanging out who call themselves celebrities, who flirt, giggle and are pretty crap singers."

John laughed … this was exactly the conversation that he hoped that Helen would start and she had played right into his hands.

"What do you think, Jackie?" said Helen, looking directly at Jackie, who was becoming increasingly uncomfortable.

"I know when it was," said Pete continuing his previous conversation. "It was fifteen years ago but I never knew why you dumped me."

Jackie once again changed the subject and said that she agreed with Helen and had told her husband that they should have some different kinds of people on John's chat show.

Pete seemed to accept this brush off but it was Bruce that revealed the truth.

"That's interesting," he said, "you must have known Jackie just before she became pregnant with Jenny."

John realised that a calamity could be about to happen if he didn't intervene and he suggested that, as it was a nice night, they might all like to sit out in the garden.

"Bruce could you help me get out the deckchairs?" John requested.

Bruce got up from his seat and followed John dutifully to the garden shed.

John and Steph's garden was only small but it was big enough for a few deckchairs. It was a warm, slightly cloudy night but the moon was trying to peek through the clouds.

"I've got some After Eights at home, Steph," said Cath, realising that John was trying to avoid a conflict. "Would you like to come and compare our house to Steph's, Jackie. I would love to show you my collection of sugars."

"I don't believe it," said Jackie, "I collect them too. Are you a member of the sucrology society?"

"Yes."

"Well, I never. You'll be telling me that you like modern art too."

"Both of us do; Carl and I were born in Birmingham and only came to Manchester twenty years ago; that's how we got talking to Steph. We hardly ever saw John and one day Steph was visiting and was hanging out some washing. We got talking and recognised her Brummy accent. Do you know Ikon Gallery?"

"Yes, I've been there a few times and went to the fortieth anniversary in July 2004."

"So did we; so you got your box of Ikon sugars then, did you?"

"Yes, but I wanted to keep the box whole and so I bought another box to share with my local sucrology group."

"They are getting on like a house on fire," said Steph to John.

"Yes, but oh dear, look at Helen and Bruce … I didn't mean to …"

"Did you know that Jackie used to be a producer too?"

"No," said John as he carried a tray of nibbles out into the back garden. "How do you find out these things?"

"I wasn't a social worker for nothing, you know," said Steph grinning incessantly. She suddenly had a pang for the life that she had left behind.

At that same moment she felt a major movement inside her as if the twins knew what she had said.

"What's the matter?" said John as he placed the tray on the rickety table that Steph had tried so many times to chuck in the tip.

"I felt the twins move."

Chapter Forty-three

"It is so hot and I feel so fat," said Steph to Lucy down the phone.

John had gone to stay with his parents for the weekend but Steph stayed at home as they had a problem with the boiler and Steph had to be there when the man came to fix it.

"You go," she said as they woke up that Friday morning, "I'll ring and get someone in."

She was very lucky that they had a cancellation but it was on Saturday morning and now she was waiting for the man to arrive. Her mobile rang.

"Hold on a mo," said Steph to Lucy, "John's on the mobile, he's probably ringing about the boiler."

"Hi, I'm talking to Lucy... no he hasn't come yet."

Steph switched the mobile off after sending kisses to John.

"So what's new?" said Steph placing the receiver back up to her ear.

"Well, I hear that Martin has got a new woman in his life."

"Oh," said Steph, "and is it anyone we know?"

"No, apparently he met her on a course; she is a social work lecturer at a university but no one seems to know where, and she has a couple of teenage kids."

"Sounds interesting."

"He's thinking about moving."

"Really; blimey, the team would be strange without Martin in it."

"Tom says that they are missing you."

"Ah, that's nice." You can tell him to tell them that I am missing them too but am enjoying being at home for a while but I feel so fat."

"So do I," said Lucy.

"You're not..."

"Yes, due in four months."

"You kept that a secret."

"Well I don't believe in telling anyone too early."

Steph remembered how she had felt when she had lost her baby soon after Alan's death. That seemed so long ago now. So many things had happened.

The doorbell rang.

"He's here, got to go, love to Tom and the kids," she said.

She went to the door and a rather tall slim man stood in front of her.

"Come in," she said, "I was lucky to get an appointment at such short notice."

He didn't take long to find the fault and as she wrote the cheque she thought about what to do next. She shut the front door, giving it that extra push. It had been stiff for ages and John said that he was going to fix it but like many other things, including the ghastly wallpaper in the dining room, it just never seemed to get done.

"I bet somebody loved that," Cath had said about the wallpaper.

"I expect they did," Steph had wondered at the time. "What were the previous people like?" Steph had asked.

"I didn't know them very well, they just kept themselves to themselves, thought that they were a bit posh, I think. Well, when he had the third stroke they decided to go and live in Wales with their daughter and, well, they never kept in touch."

Steph sat in Asda and munched her macaroni cheese and chips. She would normally have had it with salad but she felt very hungry these days.

"Eating for two?" said the elderly woman in the queue.

"No, for three," said Steph as she handed the cashier a five pound note.

"Oh lovely, twins, are they your first?"

"Yes," Steph said suddenly feeling proud that she was going to be a mum. She had bought a swimming costume and after strolling around a few shops she decided to get in the car and drive to the local pool; being a Saturday she assumed that it would all be public swimming.

"The public session starts in twenty minutes," she was told, "but you can sit through there if you like."

Steph sat in the front row of the visitors' area and watched the many children and fewer parents in the pool. They all seemed to be having a good time except for one child who just wouldn't go in the pool. She sat on the side and her dad tried to coax her into the pool.

"Hello," said someone who Steph didn't recognise. "You don't remember me?"

"Sorry."

"I work at the studio and have worked on your John's chat show. I met you a while back, when it first started."

"Oh yes, you're Kate."

"That's right; you have a good memory for names."

"No, not really, its just that I had a close friend called Kate. So, have you a child in the water?" said Steph enquiringly.

"Yes, that little girl there," she pointed at a blond-haired child aged about seven years old.

"She is with my partner Doreen."

"Oh," said Steph, realising that she was a little taken aback.

"So when is your baby due?" she said, ignoring Steph's exclamation.

"Seven weeks," said Steph.

"And how has it been?"

"Mostly fine but I'm tired quite a lot at the mo."

"So you've left John at home. Oh, and in case you were wondering, it was Doreen who had the baby. We decided to take it in turns and so I'll have the next. We have been trying but nothing has happened yet."

Kate told Steph all about the process; it seemed rather clinical to Steph and she remembered the nights of passion that she had shared with John and some afternoons too, when they would snuggle up together afterwards and talk about everyone being busy at work. It had been so wonderful. She thought of John and how for this very minute she missed him and wondered whether he missed her. At that second her phone bleeped and there was a text from John. She took it out of her bag and read the text. It said "I miss you."

Steph texted back, "I miss you too."

It felt wonderful floating on her back and as she looked up at the patterns in the ceiling she felt herself go into a trance and all at once it felt as though both Paul and Alan were lying next to her. They were telling her that she had been patient and courageous and that they were so proud of her.

"Cuckoo," said a voice. It was Jean from the antenatal class. "You seemed to be in a trance, as if you were in a world of your own," she said.

Jean was due about the same time as Steph but had carried on working. She was a social worker too, working with leaving care kids.

"Yes, I suppose I was, I was just thinking about the past."

"Oh, a dangerous pastime," said Jean, laughing. "So you're not bored at home then?" continued Jean.

"No."

"Pity."

"Why?"

"Because we are so short of staff."

"Sorry Jean, I have no plans for going back to social work for a while; besides John and I are planning to move."

"Where?"

"Oh, we're not sure but probably a village near Stafford. We both fancy bringing up the twins in a village and from Stafford you can get to most places easily on the train."

By the time Steph got home it was teatime and she decided to put a potato in the microwave. As she piled the cheese on top the phone rang.

"Hi Steph," said a muffled voice, "this is Jackie."

Steph wondered who Jackie was and then realised that it was the wife of John's producer who had come to tea a few weeks back.

Since that meal John's programmes had improved and he was a lot happier about the compromise whereby they had an equal balance between celebrities and interesting people from a variety of walks of life.

"I didn't know who to talk to," she said.

"What's up?" said Steph, becoming aware that Jackie was crying.

"It's Bruce, he's left me and has gone to live with Helen, you know, the woman that you introduced him to."

"Oh, I'm so sorry," Steph said, feeling very guilty.

"Can I come over with the kids?"

"Of course you can."

Steph barely had time to eat her baked potato and the door bell rang. She quickly took her plate and glass into the kitchen. Steph opened the door and Jackie stood with the three children on the doorstep.

"Come in," she said. "Have you had anything to eat?"

"No," all three children piped up. So Steph gave them a tenner and told them where the chippy was.

"I just couldn't believe it when I saw Pete that night," Jackie said.

"It brought back all sorts of memories, you see I was very in love with him but when I got pregnant my parents went mad and said that if I stayed with him that they would never see me again and so I had to make a choice."

"And you've regretted it ever since?"

"Oh no, I found love with Bruce."

"So what went wrong?"

"He told me that I should not have deceived him, that I should have told him the truth and that he was going to teach me a lesson. I didn't believe him at the time until he publicly started an affair with Helen and I found people laughing at me. You see our world, that of the media, can be so cruel. John is so lucky to have you who he obviously adores."

"Oh Jackie, I am so sorry, I feel so guilty."

"It's not your fault, it had to happen."

"Yoo hoo, anyone home?" Cath appeared at the back door. Steph had tried to get her to come to the front door but with no luck. Steph opened the door.

"Oh sorry, you've got visitors. Oh, it's you Jackie, how are you?"

Jackie burst into tears.

"Oh dear," said Cath putting her arms around Jackie, "Come on, it can't be that bad."

Chapter Forty-four

"We've got new neighbours," said Steph.

"Oh," said John, bringing his bag in from the car. "Mum's sent you some damson jam; she knows how you love it."

122

"Yum, I'll have some now on some ice cream. How are they anyhow?"

"Oh, blooming. Tell me about the new neighbours."

So Steph told him about the events over the weekend and how Cath and Carl had insisted that Jackie and the children move in with them.

"But they'll be rather overcrowded."

"Cath will love it, having a family to look after."

"Yes. Come here, woman of my dreams," John said, and Steph fell into his arms.

"Yoo hoo," said Cath, coming to the back door.

"Oh, I saw you were back John; how are your mum and dad?" Cath didn't give John a chance to reply before she started talking about her new family. "Oh the children are just gorgeous. Did you know that they have been bullied at school and so we were talking about them coming to Park School."

Steph laughed and wondered how long this arrangement would last.

"Just leave them be," said John.

"I will," said Steph; besides she was realising that very soon she would be too busy to help other people out.

"I want to have a social worker on the programme. Will you come on?" said John.

"Why me?"

"Because you have so much to say and because you are my wife and because I am proud of you, please?"

"It will have to be soon."

"What about tomorrow?"

"Why, has someone dropped out?"

"No," John's lie wasn't very convincing. "Well, yes... but I want you to come on anyhow, pleasie, just for me."

Steph knew that if John spoke in that way and with that look, just as he couldn't refuse her, neither could she refuse him.

"But the babes are due in two weeks."

"Pleasie."

"Oh, OK but I might give birth when I shit myself going on TV."

"I'll look after you and I will deliver you safely home afterwards," he chuckled, with a big smirk all over his face.

She knew the charms of her husband. He had won so many women over in his years and sometimes she couldn't understand why she just felt no sense of danger with so many beautiful and intelligent women passing through his life. But she didn't; she knew that he only wanted her and that she only wanted him.

That night Steph couldn't sleep; she felt that her whole life was about to change and not just because of the twins but going on TV. She was scared and excited at the same time.

John had told Bruce that he was going to have Steph on his show.

"You can't have your wife on," he said.

"Why not?"

They had a long discussion about how interesting her job had been and that she had so many things to say. But Bruce still wasn't happy about it.

"Well then, I'll leave," said John. "I'm not having her because she is my wife but because of the social work. It is time that social workers were given a voice and she says she'll do it."

"OK, but don't blame me if your marriage is ruined because of it. By the way how are Jackie and the kids? Tom said that they were staying at your neighbours' house. It appears that they think your neighbours are the best grandparents that they could ever have."

"You'll have to go and see for yourself," John said, changing the subject.

He had never really liked Bruce but the way that he had walked out on his family really peeved him.

"What, you are on tonight?" said Lucy.

"Yes, I'm so excited and scared at the same time. I can't imagine what it will be like to be interviewed by my own husband."

"You look gorgeous," said John. "We have to go."

They drove to the studio in John's Smart car and were waved through all of the security.

124

"Got to go now, Sally will look after you, love you."

Suddenly Steph was left alone with a member of the TV staff.

"Well, this is a first for us," she said, "I don't think that we've ever had a husband or wife on any of our chat shows before."

"So you don't approve," said Steph.

"I don't get a say," she said coldly.

Steph waited in the coffee lounge, where she noticed how pampered the celebrity was. She didn't know who she was as she hadn't kept up with the latest pop groups. She was just what Helen had said and had the most gorgeous figure with the low cut front which revealed what her friend Sandra would describe as the "false boobs".

"Are you girls alright?" said Bruce as he passed by.

Steph laughed to herself and the nerves that she thought might overtake her suddenly disappeared.

Floating around the room were two rather burly men.

"Who are they?" whispered Steph to Sally, who was now not so frosty.

"Her security guards," she said.

"Oh dear." It reminded Steph of Ruby. She told Sally how she knew a famous American film star and, when she mentioned her name, Sally warmed even more to her.

"I love her work."

"She offered to give her life story to John."

"Really, and will he take her up on that?"

"Doubt it, John likes to do his own thing."

"Yes we know. Your John is a great guy but we have had a few rough patches with him and Bruce arguing about who should be on the show. It's as if John would like the show to be educational, but who wants that at this time of night. People just want to be entertained."

"But surely you can have both," said Steph. "The BBC was started with that aim."

"Come on Steph, live in the real world, you are such an idealist."

"But without that idealism don't you get Big Brother and Brave New World?"

"We'll never get Big Brother from independent TV, we can't afford it," she said.

Steph realised that she meant the TV show and not the book but then Sally could only be in her mid-twenties and probably had never read it. She had been brought up with soap stars as the real royalty.

Steph knew why John had to have her on the show and what he was trying to do before it was too late.

Chapter Forty-five

"John, we have a surprise guest who wants to come on at the last minute with Steph."

"Who is it?"

"She said that she wants you to trust her and won't tell us but assures us that she is a big name."

"Is Bruce still here?"

"Nope he's gone home," said Tony.

"Let's go with it then," said John.

"I think you are mad but OK."

Steph didn't know anything that was going on in the background; the celebrity beauty went on and did her slot and Steph knew that in a few minutes it would be her turn and she began to panic. Sally realised and assured her that she would be OK.

Sally had worked for the company since she was eighteen and was waiting for a break. At twenty-eight she thought it would never happen. She had seen so many people who she thought had no talent and when she heard that John was going to bring his wife on the show she thought, "Have we really reached the bottom?" But now she met Steph she was warming to her. She had been instructed to keep her calm.

"There is another guest coming after you apparently but it's all hush hush who she is, apparently John doesn't know either."

"Oh dear, I'm not sure how he'll take that."

"Well it'll make good TV."

These words resounded in Steph's head, "It'll make good TV."

"You're on," Sally said as she pushed Steph towards the studio.

"Well, I know that this is a bit controversial but I've brought my wife on to the show, and so will you welcome Steph."

Steph walked into the bright TV lights and John gave her one of his quick cuddles and whispered, "Just be you."

John was good, he guided the discussion so she could talk freely about her days as a social worker and the concerns that she had and then John had a message in his ear.

"Well, folks it, appears that we have an extra surprise guest and so folks I would like to welcome …"

As he said her name the audience drowned out his words.

Steph couldn't believe it: there was Ruby. She had heard that Steph was going to be on and had rung the TV company to say that she wanted to come on the show. Steph hugged her.

"Well, this is a surprise. Why did you want to gatecrash my show?" said John, taking it all in good spirit, knowing that the programme would overrun and the schedulers would be mad.

"I just wanted to say a public thank you to Steph for what she has done for me and Carly and to say that I would be happy to come in with her any day to tell my story and how wonderful my social worker was. And no, I'm not here to sing a song. I know that people are waiting for the next programme."

And with that Ruby left the stage.

John quickly rounded up the show

"Wow," he said afterwards.

"Where is she?" he said, referring to Ruby.

"Oh, she left, she felt it was safer."

"What a woman," John said.

And for a brief moment Steph felt a pang of jealousy. Steph's mobile rang.

"I'm sorry if I upstaged you," Ruby said, "but I just wanted the world to know how grateful I am to you. Carly came home last week and I am just so happy. We must meet up," she said.

Steph agreed but said that she would be rather busy for a bit.

"I'm so pleased for you," she said, "and please say sorry to John."

Chapter Forty-six

All of John's fears were misguided. The press was full of it and suddenly took an unusual interest in social work. Over the next two weeks they managed to get all sorts of people on the show, with homeless people who had made good sitting next to ones who were picked up off the street.

Bruce, although initially annoyed, was now over the moon but Steph was concerned it was getting out of hand and was becoming rather a freak show.

"I don't know how to stop it," John said

"They'll get bored," said Ruby. "It'll settle down, you'll see. So where are these babies then?"

"Must be boys," Steph said implying that boys were lazier than girls.

"So do you have any names?"

"Not really, we'll just see what they look like."

Ruby laughed.

Steph swam every day. It made her weight feel less of a burden for a short time. But getting dressed afterwards was becoming increasingly difficult.

She had had false alarms for about a week and every night when she went to bed she expected to have to wake John and go hurtling off to the hospital.

Since the programme she had become a minor celebrity and was amused by anyone taking any level of interest in her.

Bruce and Jackie had made it up but the kids still came round to see their adoptive grandparents and insisted on remaining at the school even though it was two bus rides away from their home.

"We could always stay with Gran and Grandad," Steph heard the oldest say one day. This made her laugh but it seemed to keep Cath occupied and the yoo hoos at the back door became more infrequent.

The day it happened was just an ordinary day. She wasn't at the pool or in the middle of town and John was not a hundred miles away. No, he was busy writing in his study.

"Its finished," he said, "ready for you to read in hospital."

"What is?" said Steph, pushing whites into the washing machine with great difficulty

"My novel."

"Ouch," she said. "Oh, that was bloody awful."

"We've got a girl and a boy," said John as he rang Steph's parents on the mobile. The girl came first and then the boy and they are both fine. Both were nearly seven pounds. They are going to be Lottie and Jack."

Steph was just so glad it was over. She had a few stitches, that was all, and although she was very tired she felt so happy and tomorrow she would be going home.

That night she watched the TV from her bed and suddenly there was a photo of the babies on and the ward erupted.

"Fame at last," said the sister.

Steph heard these words and wondered what world her children would be brought up in. Two innocent children who had parents in two very different working worlds.

"We must write the TV series," said Steph as John sat holding Lottie while she cuddled Jack.

"Yes," said John but not yet; for now we will just enjoy the babes.